"Tight suspense and ͵
characters make Jean B

...ـﺟ + ½ **of 5 stars**

Discover the third book in New York Times bestselling Texas romance author Jean Brashear's TEXAS HEROES: Lone Star Lovers series about three brothers, this story a uniquely powerful reunion romance between a haunted detective and the woman whose life he once saved.

FBI agent Alex Sandoval has never forgiven himself for not protecting a young girl who was gravely injured and her mother killed before her eyes during his first hostage negotiation twelve years ago. Now Jade Butler is a cop herself, assigned to a prestigious multi-agency task force hunting for the killer of several young girls in Austin, Texas—and Alex is the agent in charge of the case.

They never met all those years ago, but Jade recognizes his voice as the one she still hears in her dreams, the voice that has comforted her through many a terrifying flashback. Her role on the task force is undercover, serving as bait for a madman, yet Alex cannot stop trying to protect her as he was unable to do years ago. Tensions ratchet between them as old memories vie with a powerful new attraction, and when Jade is taken hostage by the killer, it's Alex's worst nightmare as he must negotiate once again—only this time, it's to save the woman he loves.

A rewriting of a story once called Most Wanted

Texas Protector

Texas Heroes: Lone Star Lovers
Book 3
(Texas Heroes 21)

Jean Brashear

Prologue

Austin
Twelve years ago

S wollen with summer's heat, droplets of orange streetlight tumbled through the darkness. Eyes closed, Alejandro Sandoval zeroed his focus on the nightmare playing out in the bedroom less than a hundred yards away.

With effort, he ignored flashing police lights, gawkers jostling the cordon, adrenaline boiling through the SWAT team surrounding him. Violence stamped its feet, eager to breach the apartment where a terrified young girl fought for her mother's life…and her own.

To his left, the SWAT commander muttered into his headset. Alex had only a few moments more to salvage this situation before it would be ripped from his hands. The commander's contempt for hostage negotiation was crystal-clear. His men were ready to rock, and Alex did not have the authority to hold them back.

His shirt clung to his spine in damp patches. His first solo negotiation, and the hostage taker had refused to speak to him anymore.

A frightened fifteen-year-old girl was Alex's only hope, and he was hers. If he failed…

He swallowed, his mouth raspy and dust-dry. He cleared

his throat, took a sip of water and dialed again.

"H-hello?"

Steady. She's all you've got.

"Jade, if he's standing right beside you, just say *pardon me*."

The only sound was her rapid breathing.

"Good for you," he said. "Are you hurt?"

"No," she whispered.

"Is your mother worse?" What little he'd been able to piece together from the 911 recording indicated that Jade Butler's mother had met the hopped-up ex-con named Kirk Claypool in a bar that night, and the girl had been awakened by her mother's agonized cries as Claypool beat Belle Butler behind a locked door.

"She's—" Her voice broke on a sob.

"What's he asking?" Claypool roared in the background.

"You're doing fine," Alex soothed. It wasn't a lie. The girl had maintained her composure well beyond what anyone would expect of someone her age. "We'll get her help. Everything's going to work out." Beside him, the SWAT commander tensed and cursed.

"Tell him I've got new information. Ask him again if he'll speak to me." Time was running out.

He heard her quick inhalation, as if she sought yet again to settle her nerves. Fifteen. She should be giggling on the phone with some boy, not struggling to survive while a maniac freaked about going back to prison, screamed demands and battered her mother.

How long before he started in on Jade, too?

"He's got something new to tell you. He wants to know if you'll talk to him this time," she repeated to her captor.

"There's nothing to say until I see that goddamn van out front."

The SWAT commander's fist pumped in triumph as a van

rolled up. He caught Alex's eye. Time was up. No more negotiations. The tactical phase of this operation was under way.

Alex had only one more duty: to lure the captor to the window.

He squeezed his eyes shut as he cast about for a last-ditch means to get the man back on the phone. To salvage the situation before the bullets began flying.

The commander grabbed his shoulder and glared. With a cutting motion, he ended Alex's hope of doing anything but preparing Jade to protect herself.

Failure lay bitter on Alex's tongue, but he shoved away every thought save protecting this courageous young girl. "Jade, tell him to look outside. The van is here. You be alert and stay down. Avoid the window, but don't fight him. If he tries to take you to the window, go limp and fall."

"The van's out there." She relayed and muffled a sob.

"You come with me, goddamn it," Kirk growled.

Alex heard her gasp in pain.

The phone clattered to the floor.

"Jade—" Alex mentally reached out to stop her, but he knew it was too late.

Black-garbed men fanned around the building. Up the stairs.

Deadly snipers took aim.

Alex wanted to crush his headphones into the grimy pavement. To charge inside. Shield her. Things shouldn't have reached this point. He should have—

"Please—" Jade's plea, instantly stifled.

A slap. "*Now*, I said!"

A low moan.

"Mama—"

"I'll kill you both, girl—"

Alex's eyes locked on the window. Every second was an hour.

A glimpse of long red hair wreathing a very young, stricken face.

A man's hand clenched around her vulnerable throat.

Down, Jade. Fall. Please…dear God, let her—

Jade collapsed.

Her captor's pistol rose, aimed at her—

Shots rang out.

Screams in Alex's earphones—

"Mama, no—"

Shattering glass—

Crashing wood—

"Please—" Jade's cry was so faint. "Help me—"

Alex clutched his headset so tightly it cracked. "Jade—" he shouted.

"We're in. Three casualties. Get the paramedics—quick," the team leader snapped.

Alex hurled his equipment to the ground and raced toward the girl he should have been able to save.

Chapter One

Present day

Austin police detective Jade Butler strode down the hallway of the nondescript office building, aware that she'd find only a suite number to indicate the headquarters of VICTAF, the elite FBI-funded Violent Crimes Task Force to which she'd gained temporary admission.

She swiped the key card she'd been issued; then, drawing a deep breath, she grasped the handle of the door to the most exclusive club in town.

Whatever she had expected, it looked like any squad room she'd ever inhabited—except for walls painted a color she'd have to call mauve. And carpet. Flowered carpet. She grinned, wondering who'd occupied this space before VICTAF.

The unoccupied metal desks weren't quite as beat-up as the ones she'd left in APD Sex Crimes, but they were every bit as mismatched. When she sniffed the bitter scent of over-cooked cop coffee, it eased the tension in her shoulders a little more.

Where was everyone? She glanced at her watch. Of course she was early. She was always early.

She couldn't help her eagerness. VICTAF had been operating for six years, a joint effort by Austin-area law enforcement agencies, federal, state and local, to tackle cases beyond the scope of any one of them. Some personnel, such as FBI agent and founder Doc Romero, remained constant while others rotated in and out. Slots were coveted by personnel in every agency.

Hers wasn't a permanent assignment, but it was the kind of work she'd been aiming to do ever since a madman had held her at gunpoint and killed her mother right before her eyes.

At that instant, Jade heard a male voice. Light spilled into the hallway from the office farthest down on the left. The man sounded like Doc. Jade decided not to wait—never hurt to let the boss know you were gung-ho.

Just shy of the door, she noted another voice and hesitated. The second voice seemed oddly familiar. From the tone of their voices the men seemed to be merely visiting, so she moved forward.

"You planning a trip back home any time soon, Alex?" Doc asked.

"If I don't, they'll be on my doorstep." The other man chuckled. "I'm surprised they've waited this long."

Hearing him clearly now, Jade froze in mid-step.

Him. That voice. The one from the night when—

You're doing fine…Jade, if he's standing right beside you—

Impossible. How could—She shook her head, struggling to breathe again. To think.

Surely she was imagining things.

He spoke again. "It's great to be back in Austin after so long on the East Coast."

Back. In Austin. The place where—

Before she realized it, she'd crossed the last few feet.

Doc looked up. "Good morning, Detective." His dark eyes were kind as he circled the desk to shake her hand. He topped her by several inches, though at five eight, she was not small herself.

Jade returned his greeting, but her attention swerved to the man rising to his feet behind Doc. She stared. She'd never known her savior's name, never seen his face.

"Want a cup of coffee?" Doc asked.

She jolted. "No, thank you," she managed. She dragged her gaze back to Doc, who filled the doorway. "Thank you again, sir, for requesting me. I'll do you a good job."

"If I didn't believe that, you wouldn't be here." He moved back to let her enter. "Jade Butler, this is Alex Sandoval, also FBI," Doc said. "We stole him from D.C. recently."

Alex. His name was Alex.

Jade saw a man, probably late thirties, whose face was both handsome and severe, his bone structure dramatic and arresting. Over six feet in height, powerful build. Hair a glossy crow's-wing black, ruthlessly trimmed to control curls that wouldn't quite be tamed. Eyes more golden than brown.

Frowning, he extended a hand.

She held out her own, jittery about hearing him speak again. When his hand clasped hers firmly, a quick, involuntary shiver raced over her skin.

"Butler?" His face was carefully neutral, his eyes gone blank and still.

She swallowed hard and forced a nod. "Yes. Jade Butler."

"Jade," he repeated slowly. "I—" He glanced away, then back. "Pleased to meet you."

The sound of her name on his lips sealed it.

Dear God. She'd know it anywhere, that voice. She'd listened to it a thousand times in her dreams. It had woven itself into the fabric of her soul, the warp and woof of the darkest day of her life. Salvation. Terror. Comfort. Despair.

What was he doing here? FBI, had Doc said? If he remembered her, what would that mean for her job here? No one in the department knew—

Doc was looking at her oddly. *Pull it together, Jade.* "I...same here."

"Why don't you have a seat and we'll catch you up," Doc said.

She grasped the arm of her chair and sank into it. "Thanks," she somehow answered, folding her shaking hands in her lap.

It can't be. Alex settled back heavily in his seat, his mind racing to catch up. What was she doing here? How could she be a cop?

She was forever fifteen and terrified when he woke in a cold sweat. He tried to concentrate on what Doc was saying, but that night never went away easily, no matter how spotless his record since. His supervisor had assured him that the fault was not his, that the incident commander had rushed the tactical solution when negotiations should have continued. It didn't help; Alex had examined each second over and over, poring for the misstep that had paved the way for disaster.

He'd promised her everything would work out right.

She'd trusted him to deliver.

He'd been her lifeline, her route out of a nightmare, and because he hadn't done his job well enough, she had a picture in her memory that would never vanish.

Or from his.

She'd been gone in an ambulance by the time he'd been allowed inside the apartment, but he'd seen the blood everywhere. Her screams still echoed in his head in the solitary hours of the night.

The cops who'd stormed the apartment had found her wounded by gunshot, cradling her mother in her arms and pleading for her to wake up, to open her eyes. To stay with a child suddenly cast into the world alone. She'd refused to let go until officers had pried her mother from her arms and delivered Jade to the paramedics.

Word had come down that she'd wanted to meet the negotiator during those dark days following her rescue. He hadn't been sorry to get caught up in another case. Before he'd had a chance to figure out the right words of apology, her grandparents had whisked her away to Oklahoma. To his everlasting shame, Alex had been relieved. He'd tried his damnedest to bury it.

But some cases you never forgot.

Did she know who he was?

And what on earth could he say to her if she did?

He shot her a sideways glance and saw her gaze fastened on him for only an instant before she jerked her attention back to Doc.

The name was the same. The red hair, the enormous mossy green eyes.

A cop. Could the frightened teenager have become a cop?

"Alex, you got anything from your CI?" Doc's question yanked him right back to the present.

"Sore feet," he managed.

Doc's grin was wry. Alex saw her smile faintly, too. Confidential informants were a common bane for cops.

"He'll show up today with some great excuse for why he wasn't where he said he'd be. His tales are some of my best entertainment."

"I prefer the X-rated kind myself." Bob Jordan of Alcohol, Tobacco and Firearms stepped in from the hallway, coffee cup in hand. "Oops. Didn't know a lady was present."

"No lady," Jade responded as she rose and held out her hand. "Just another cop. Jade Butler, APD."

"Bob Jordan, ATF. Been with Doc since the beginning of

VICTAF." He shook her hand while his gaze scanned her figure. "Nice change of scenery. Ever let that hair down, Red?"

Alex stifled the urge to tell Bob to go easy.

She didn't blink an eye. "Why? You need some?"

Bob laughed and smoothed fingers over his rapidly thinning hair. "Wouldn't match. But thanks for the offer."

She handled herself well, trading banter without taking offense. This Jade Butler had come a long way, a woman, cool and self-possessed. Her attire was stark and simple. The vulnerable eyes he remembered looked different in the face of a confident woman. They topped an aquiline nose and an unpainted, generous mouth that fit her name far more than the image she obviously wanted. Her auburn hair was scraped tightly into a braid coiled into a bun at the back of her neck, yet somehow the severe style only emphasized her good bones. Her carriage was proud, the metamorphosis complete. The frail girl was nowhere in sight.

Alex reminded himself that for Doc to pick her, she had to be both experienced and competent. She didn't need him running interference.

"Okay, let's move on," Doc said. "We've got a new investigation on tap. Alex, I want you heading it."

Alex nodded.

"APD has asked for our help. Lots of political pressure coming to bear on this one. Three young women have disappeared from the Sixth Street entertainment district. These are all coeds at the university, two freshmen and one sophomore, who, for different reasons, arrived alone at the bars. Two were coming to meet friends. We don't know why the other was there by herself."

"Stupid," muttered Bob.

Doc grimaced. "Yeah, but they're young. It's Sixth Street

in Austin, they're from Podunk, Texas, and Mama and Daddy are far away, so they're not too worried about anything but fun in a town renowned for great music and good times. And because Sixth Street has been relatively safe, no one's thinking that anything really bad could happen to them. I mean, it's not New York or L.A., right?"

He glanced at each one of them. "The two meeting friends each arrives—APD knows that from showing around pictures at the bar—but never hooks up with her buddies. Friends assume she just didn't make it, then finally report her missing a day, maybe two after. The third girl was reported by her parents three days later, after she failed to call home for her father's birthday."

"What's the connection?" Alex asked.

"Time of night and Sixth Street bars are the only common elements right now," Doc answered. "Height of the late-night rush when most patrons have been drinking for a while. Bar staff are overloaded. Two different clubs, alternating. Each one with lots of noise, plenty of low lighting and convenient nooks."

"How far apart?" Bob asked.

"Three days each time. First and third disappearances happened at the same bar."

"Any physical description of who they encountered?" Alex queried.

"Nothing consistent. Staff at the first club was too busy to notice who the girl talked to. At the second, a waitress remembers that night's girl flirting with several men, but no one stuck with her."

"Video capability in any of them?" Alex asked.

"First club, Wild Child, has a camera on the sidewalk in front," Doc said. "Second club is called Night Dreams. No video inside or out."

Alex was certain that everyone present was on the same page he was. This would be an undercover job, and only one person in the room had the critical qualifications. "That why Butler is here?" His voice sounded harsh, even to his own ears.

Doc frowned, then nodded. "Jade has done a lot of undercover work on the Sex Crimes unit."

Alex already didn't like it. "She's not in her teens."

Doc studied her. "You're twenty-seven, but you could pass for younger, especially with your hair down."

She shrugged. "I still get carded."

Doc smiled at her obvious disgust.

"Don't knock it, kid," Bob put in. "My wife would kill to have someone card her."

"You up for this, Jade?" Doc asked. "Nothing like jumping from the frying pan into the fire."

"I'm here to work," she said. "I know the club scene. I can start tonight, see what happens."

"That's up to Alex." Doc turned back to Alex. "I'd suggest Sean"

Alex nodded. "He's got a baby face that gets him carded, too."

"You pick who you need to round out a team. APD's getting serious heat from both university and business interests. South by Southwest is coming up in two weeks, and the various festivals bring thousands of visitors, many of them this age group, and tons of money into the local economy. Lots of media attention. Sixth Street needs to be safe before then."

Alex concurred absently. He was having trouble making the leap from a fifteen-year-old with a gun to her head to a woman eager to serve as bait. He'd have to pull her jacket, check her out.

And talk to Doc.

"Bob, ask Sarge to start making a list of female patrol officers with undercover experience. I want options."

"You got it," Bob responded.

Jade frowned.

He ignored it. "And Doc, I'd like a word with you."

Doc nodded. "Sure. I have to make one call first."

Alex headed for the coffeepot, studiously ignoring the eyes he could feel boring into his back. He took his time pouring the brew that could walk on its own. Then he headed back to Doc's office, swearing as he burned his tongue.

But she was waiting in the hall. "Do you—" She halted, a flash of vulnerability in her eyes, just as quickly gone.

He remained silent.

A faint line appeared between slender brows. He could see, up close, that she wore no makeup. The rosy lips were her own. They clearly didn't belong to a child.

The generous mouth tightened. "You requested other choices." She studied him, the frown deepening. "I can hold my own. Ask anyone."

He waited to see if she would make reference to the past. Maybe he'd lucked out and she didn't know who he was. He'd never forget her, but she'd been young. Twelve years ago, almost half her life. Back when he'd been cocky and sure of himself, same age she was now.

"Doc requested me because I'm good." Her jaw flexed. "Let me prove it."

He imagined it had cost her to ask. Her poise was something he remembered from that night; though he'd heard the terror in her voice, she'd kept her wits. Months later, he'd slipped into the back of the courtroom as she testified against her captor. Even then, bone white with fear, facing the man who'd shattered her world, she'd had a composure far beyond her years.

This woman who'd been a girl he'd let down so badly was only asking him to be fair. He owed her a debt he could never repay.

Did he really want to find out if she remembered him? Discuss that night? Absolutely not.

But he also never wanted to be responsible for her again.

"I'll be going over your record," he said, watching her eyes. She held firm. "Everything checks out you're on the team. I don't like what I see, Doc or no Doc, you're out—got that?"

"If this is because—" She seemed to reconsider, her cheeks bright spots of color. "I'll pass muster." If he'd been tinder, he'd have burst into flames from the temper in her eyes.

"You so sure?"

The air hummed with tension.

Finally, she spoke, her voice ice-cold. "There's nothing in my file that will cause a problem, *sir.*"

He met her gaze squarely. She didn't look away. "I can do the job, Agent Sandoval. And I want this chance."

He saw the pride, the control, the strength. She probably *was* good. Doc wouldn't accept anything less. And since she was the victim and not the criminal in a case, she was likely right that he wouldn't find anything in her file about that night. But would Doc have selected her if he'd known?

Alex had to admire her spunk. "I don't want any cowboys on my team, Detective. I'll be watching every move you make. I yank your leash, you stop on a dime."

Her eyes shot sparks, but she nodded. "You're the case agent."

"Remember that." He walked away.

Doc met him at the door. "I've got a meeting in five

minutes. What's up?"

Alex glanced toward the woman who'd once been a thin, frightened girl.

He turned to Doc. "Never mind. It can wait."

Doc slapped him on the back. "I'm glad you were interested in relocating closer to your family, Alex. I'm aware that they tried to keep you in D.C., but we need a good head like yours."

"Thanks, Doc," Alex said. "I'm glad to be here, too." At least he had been.

Right up until the moment he'd laid eyes on Jade Butler.

Jade observed him from the break room, her stomach queasy. He acted as though they were strangers. True, twelve years had elapsed. To be certain he was the one, there were only two avenues: go after the old case file and risk unveiling herself—or ask him.

Neither appealed.

Maybe she was wrong. There would be nothing to worry about if he wasn't—

No. All she had to do was hear him talk, and something deep inside her *knew*. Just knew.

So what now?

A part of her yearned to speak of that night, to commune with the other half of a terrible and bittersweet intimacy she'd shared with no other person on this earth.

She couldn't reconcile the man before her with the hero or the hard-nosed cop. To confront him when she wasn't sure of his reaction…

No.

How easily he'd unearthed the tongue-tied teenager she'd thought long banished. He wasn't anything like she'd imagined in all the years since that night. In her girlish dreams, he'd been big and broad and kindly, with arms strong enough to hold her close, to protect her from the nightmares. Cuddly and soothing, not cold and edgy. Not lean and handsome and dangerous.

The disconnect she felt unnerved her. She'd put a lot of distance between the helpless girl she'd once been and the competent woman she was now. Damned if she'd let him continue throwing her off stride.

She straightened, jerked her gaze from his back and pondered how to vault the hurdle he presented. It wasn't as if she didn't have practice surmounting obstacles. She'd fought hard to make a future very different from her past, and she hadn't done that by abandoning caution. Her way was to plan carefully, moving only when she was sure of the next step, and in doing so, she'd accomplished every goal she'd ever set for herself.

Her heart clenched at the thought of her losing this incredible opportunity at VICTAF. He could cost her that, this Alex Sandoval; she had to see him as he was now, not as some childish fantasy of a knight in shining armor. That being the case, she'd better proceed slowly until she knew how best to handle him.

In the meantime, she'd focus on proving herself invaluable. That settled, she veered off to find her desk.

Chapter Two

Alex let himself in the Chinese-red front door of the house he'd rented under protest. Friends of his sister-in-law Diana's had insisted that he'd be doing them a favor. The timing was all wrong to put it on the market, and they didn't want to leave it empty.

The neighborhood, so cozy and small-town feeling, wasn't his usual. And he didn't need a whole house to himself. An apartment would have been fine, since he spent most of his time working, anyway. But the location was convenient—close in, easy to get to the office.

The sunroom, though, had sold him. The light in there was incredible. After so many years of faking natural light in the tiny extra bedrooms of nondescript apartments, his having a place like that to paint in had tipped the balance. Not that he'd be home often enough to use it, but…man, what light.

Alex moved across wood floors that glowed from the couple's tender care and wondered how the place had looked when they'd lived here. Probably a hell of a lot more furnished, he imagined, glancing at the long leather sofa, lone recliner and shelves filled with television, sound system and his brother's pottery. Cartons of books still waited to be opened. The walls were bare, though he had plenty of paintings to fill them.

But he didn't display his work, ever. Only the pieces given to family left his studio. Exhibition wasn't their purpose.

In the kitchen, he opened the refrigerator. Vaguely hungry, he stared at the emptiness and made a mental note to shop for groceries.

Just as quickly, he discarded it. Anything fresh would rot before he got to it. Until this case was solved, he'd be doing the same thing he'd done tonight: ordering in or grabbing a bite on the run.

His stomach growled, and he glanced at the clock. Twelve-thirty. He'd snagged a couple of slices of the pizza Bob had ordered, but that had been hours ago. He wasn't hungry enough, though, to order out.

Alex grabbed a beer. He'd declined Bob's earlier invitation to his favorite bar in favor of reading through the rest of the case files to prepare for tomorrow's meeting of the team he'd assembled. Bob was a good guy, however, Alex wasn't a social type under optimum circumstances.

These were anything but.

And with that acknowledgment, the source of his agitation roared to center stage.

Jade Isabel Butler, former fifteen-year-old hostage, victim of a deranged killer and an incident commander with an itchy trigger finger.

And a negotiator who'd blown his job. Thanks to him, she would never be able to erase the memory of her mother dying before her eyes.

Alex slammed the beer bottle down on the tile counter, shattering it, slicing his thumb. He watched the bright red blood welling up, dripping on the pale oak floor, and he did nothing.

Damn it. If only Doc had asked him first. If only he'd known that she wasn't safely tucked away in Oklahoma

anymore. If only—

Putting that night to bed had required years, and now, as though only hours had passed, it was back.

She was back. And he was supposed to place her in harm's way.

He couldn't. Wouldn't.

But green eyes held him. Challenged him.

Pleaded with him. *Let me prove it.*

Alex closed his hand into a fist. Blood dripped through clenched fingers, and he winced at the sting.

He blew out a gust of air, then shook his head and grabbed a towel.

He jerked her braid, and her scalp burned. All around her, the room pulsed red, her hand sticky with blood, the noises so loud, so—

Then gentle hands undid her braid, fingers separating the strands, sliding through her hair . . . caressing . . .

Jade, *the voice said.* I'm here. Don't be afraid. I'm with you.

She began to relax into his touch—

I'll kill her if you screw up! *Her mother's face lined with pain, filled with fear—the night exploding into shouts and screams—her mother's body and all the blood—*

Jade's alarm shrilled. She jerked upright in the bed, her heart beating trip-hammer fast in the darkness.

She switched on the light. Five a.m. Time to head for the gym.

A dream. Just a dream.

She hadn't had one of these in a long time.

It was him. Meeting the man who belonged to that voice

had caused this.

Jade rose from her bed and padded to the bathroom to brush her teeth. In the mirror, she gazed absently at her reflection, her hair disordered and loose.

Maybe she still got carded, but she felt a thousand years old.

I'll be going over your record, he'd said. He'd appeared angry. Why?

She'd been so excited only one day earlier. A new job, her big chance. Jade had worked hard to overcome the stain of her past, to put the terror behind her. She'd survived the cold and empty years with her very proper, disapproving grandparents. Been valedictorian of her high school class.

She'd finished college in three years, attending nonstop— all her energies had been funneled into one goal: to be a cop, to save others as she'd been saved. Then, over her grandparents' protests, she'd moved back to Austin six years ago, her heart in her throat, and applied to the Academy. She'd been accepted into the next class.

And gradually, the town had come to seem like home in a way she'd never experienced with her mother. They'd always been one step ahead of the bill collectors, often moving when rent was due. Her mother had tried her best, but she'd been woefully unprepared for life as a single parent with no real job skills. Jade had a much better sense now of just how scared her mom must have been.

But Belle Butler had picked up the wrong man one lonely night, and it had been the last mistake she'd ever make.

Jade picked up no one. She worked…and she worked. She read a lot of books and cleaned her duplex…and worked some more. Every extra shift she was offered, every assignment, no matter how tough.

VICTAF was her reward, and no one was going to take

that away.

She donned on the baggy T-shirt and shorts she wore to the department gym, then quickly braided her hair, leaving the braid hanging down her back. Grabbed an apple off the counter to eat as she drove, hoping that a good exercise session would help her start getting her head on straight.

Alex swung at the punching bag hanging before him. He'd pulled her file, and just as she'd promised, there was nothing in it but superlatives. Commendations, glowing performance reviews, the whole bit.

Not one word, however, about the night that had changed her life.

And his.

Grinding his teeth, he broke into a flurry of shots at the bag.

"Whoa, Slick, who you trying to kill?"

Alex glanced up to see Doc standing nearby. Doc might be fifty-four, but he exercised almost as often as Alex.

Doc frowned. "You don't look so hot."

Alex stilled the bag's swinging. "Another long night."

"Those can be hard on a man. You gonna make it?"

Alex grinned. "Grab some gloves and we'll see."

Doc shook his head, chuckling. "Me, I'm strictly a street fighter."

Doc's misspent youth was the stuff of legend. He'd often acknowledged that but for the grace of God and a cop who cared, he'd be in prison right now. Instead, he'd decided to follow in the cop's footsteps, and the rest was history.

Doc waved at a new arrival.

Alex frowned when he saw Jade Butler arriving. Doc had been right. She appeared very young without her tailored camouflage.

"What did you need to talk to me about yesterday?" Doc asked.

Alex wanted to tell him. Probably should. But as it was on the tip of his tongue to say something, her face rose before him, a plea shadowing the fierce determination in her gaze.

"What do you know about Butler?"

Doc frowned. "You worried about her?"

Alex felt her eyes on him and caught the faint line of vulnerability in her frame as she saw them standing together, talking.

"She's young to be where she is," was all he said.

Doc nodded. "A little, but she's busted her buns to get there. Good judgment is what I keep hearing. Sound instincts." Then he frowned. "You got a problem with having her on the team?"

Alex rested his gloved hands on his hips and stared across the room at her. He shook his head slowly. "I don't know."

"Attracted, is that it?"

Alex recoiled. "I don't rob cradles."

"She's not a kid. Bettina was nine years younger than me."

Doc's wife had died a year ago, and the couple had had no children. Everyone on VICTAF knew that he mourned her still.

"It's not that." Alex shook his head. "I just—" He exhaled. Finally, he settled for a version of the truth. "I never like using women as bait."

"Sir Galahad, huh?" Doc teased. "Seventeen years on the job and you still got a white knight thing going?" His voice turned somber. "I don't want anyone on a case who can't give his all to it. If you want out, just say so. Bob can take it."

But Jade stays was the message. She had the appearance and the skills.

Alex finished what he started. "I don't." *I can't protect her if I'm not involved.*

And that was the crux of the problem. After twelve years, realization hit; he was still trying to protect a scared young girl, seeking absolution for his mistake.

But life was seldom that clean or accommodating.

And the girl had grown up.

Doc slapped him on the shoulder. "Good. You're the best man for the job." With a quick squeeze, he ambled away.

Alex looked back at the last place he'd seen her. She was stretching in front of the mirror, leaning over at the waist and bringing her head close enough to touch her knees, revealing a very shapely backside and long, firmly muscled legs.

She was definitely not a teenager anymore.

Then she straightened, and her eyes sought him in the mirror.

For a very long moment, they both stood motionless.

When her gaze left his and traveled down his body, Alex was more than surprised to feel himself stir. He muttered a curse and returned to the bag. He threw a punch so hard that the impact sang up his arm. *Serves you right*, he thought grimly. He forced himself to forget everything around him.

So intent was his concentration that when he felt the touch on his shoulder, he whirled instantly—

And barely missed throwing a punch in her face. "What the—"

"Sorry." She held up her hands, green eyes wide. "I deliberately came from the side so that you'd see me."

"I didn't." He knew he sounded too harsh, but he was still trying to level out the adrenaline firing through his system. He exhaled sharply. "What's up?"

"Would you like to spar a bit on the mat?"

He cocked his head. "Why?"

"You need to understand that I can take care of myself, that I'm the best person for the job."

He shrugged. "Doc says you are."

"But do *you* believe it?"

"I'll take your word."

Jade snorted. "I doubt that. What is it? Don't like fighting women?"

Not when they're you, he had the urge to say, but he was aware of the absurdity of feeling protective. He never liked sending women into danger, but that didn't mean he hadn't done it.

He had to get past this. They must work together some-how. "All right." He brought one glove up to his teeth to untie it.

"Here—" Jade stepped forward, grasped his glove and brought it near. "Let me help."

She was only inches away, her head bent in concentration, his glove nestled almost between her breasts as she used both hands to unlace it with fingers that were long and graceful and deft. She was close enough for him to breathe in the scent of her, a totally feminine mix that wafted past the gym odors and left him smelling cinnamon and peaches. He could see the tender pink of her scalp where she'd parted her hair to braid it, the faint dusting of freckles across her nose.

Alex gritted his teeth and looked away, all the while curs-ing himself that she provoked such mixed reactions in him. She wouldn't welcome any of them.

"Are you finished?" If he could walk out without having to explain, he'd leave the gym right now.

"Almost." The tip of her tongue worried at her full lower lip as she concentrated. Desire punched him right in the gut.

The second she let go, Alex jerked his hand away.

"Want me to do the other one?"

"No." Hell, no. One had been more than enough. "I'll be right back." He yanked off the glove and walked toward his bag while he unlaced the other one.

"Okay." He returned. "You ready?"

Finished removing her shoes, she nodded and strode to the middle of the mat.

"No pads?" he asked.

"Nope."

He shrugged, removed his second shoe and sock and approached her.

They circled each other for a few moments, assessing. Just about the time Alex thought she might dither forever, she struck out with a lightning-fast kick to his head. He ducked it and turned. "No pulling punches, eh?"

Competition gleamed in her eyes. "Should I?" She shrugged. "I mean, you're what, forty?"

"Thirty-nine." His brows rose. "And I hope you've got more than trash talk in your arsenal."

Her smile was thin. "Oh, I do." She whirled and tried to come in under his guard.

He responded too cautiously, and she moved on dancer's feet to lever his arm and flip him over her hip. He landed flat on his back.

"Stop treating me like a girl." Her eyes shot sparks.

Alex leaped to his feet easily. She wasn't fifteen anymore, and she was good. Playing Galahad would only get him embarrassed.

"Don't worry," he said grimly. "It won't happen again."

The battle was joined in earnest. For several minutes, they sparred, and he had to admire her grace, her economy of motion. She was toned to a greater degree than he'd realized.

What she lacked in brute strength, she compensated for in speed and cunning. Twice more, she almost got the better of him.

In the end, he won, but she made him work for it.

Alex extended his hand to her as she lay on the mat, fury barely contained. He could see the temptation simmering.

"Don't even think about it," he warned.

Her eyes narrowed. Finally, she clasped his hand, barely requiring the help to leap lightly to her feet. She shrugged. "I hate to lose."

"You almost didn't."

"I want a rematch."

"Give me a few days, all right? I'm an old man."

She gave a decidedly unladylike snort and grinned. This close, he realized that her skin was nearly translucent. What pigments would he mix to attempt to paint that?

Alex sobered abruptly. He shouldn't be noticing her skin. Or her figure. "I have to go. Good match." She'd proven her point—she could defend herself. He had to leave—now—before he got any more confused by all that she stirred in him.

Emotions got people killed. He would not endanger anyone under his command.

Especially not her.

Without looking back, he walked out.

"Hey, Jade, wait up—"

She was halfway up the first set of stairs at VICTAF. She turned and saw Sean Fitzgerald cover two steps at a time behind her. "Hi," she said.

"Hi. Glad to see someone else tackle the stairs besides

Alex and me. You should hear Bob huff and puff when Alex bullies him into doing it."

Jade smiled. "I like Bob."

"Me, too. That's why we want to keep him healthy." He reached her step and stopped. Probably six feet with tawny hair and calm gray eyes, he appeared very fit.

Like Alex. *Sandoval*, she corrected. Agent Sandoval. Your *boss*.

But Alex's muscles were the thicker ones of a mature man. Mature, yet far from old. The image of him this morning—powerful, glistening with sweat—wouldn't go away.

Lord have mercy. Clad in a sweat-soaked ancient T-shirt with no sleeves, armholes torn out halfway down to his waist, he was devastating. Delectable. Female eye candy. Those gorgeous Latin looks were plenty when he was fully dressed, but in his gym clothes, she could see how strong he was, his arms, shoulders and torso ripped with the kind of definition that made her mouth go dry.

Couple that with a trim waist and long, muscular legs, and Jade had fought the urge to fan herself.

Ridiculous to feel that way. Alex Sandoval was hardly the first man she'd worked out with. She spent her days surrounded by males.

But none of them looked like that one.

She wasn't a teenager with a crush anymore, damn it. And how this man viewed her professionalism would weigh heavily on her future in VICTAF. That was why she'd challenged him to spar in the first place. He could be an obstacle or an asset. How events played out was up to her. She'd needed a few minutes, but she'd finally gotten past his physical presence.

She liked what she sensed of Sean and decided to hazard a chance. "Tell me about Sandoval. He got a problem working with women?"

"We go by first names here. To answer your question, Alex's just overprotective. He hasn't been here that long, yet it's easy to see that he takes responsibility very seriously. More so with women and kids, still, he came on like a big brother to me right away. Wanted to tell him I already have two of them at home, but hey—he's got seniority. One day he reveals that he's got three younger siblings. Probably can't help himself." Then his eyebrows rose. "You know who one of his brothers is? Liam Sullivan."

Jade blinked. "The actor?"

"Yep."

Jade had just seen his latest box office hit. He'd played a cop very convincingly. No wonder. "Wow. He's—" *Hot.* More than hot.

Sean laughed. "Women. I don't get what's so great about him. I mean, I like his films and all, but he's just a guy."

His peevish tone made her chuckle. "Women all over the world would argue with you." Then she frowned. "Why don't they have the same last name?"

"Doc says they're half brothers. Same mother but different dads. Alex's father died and his mom remarried."

"I guess he's proud of having a famous kid brother."

"He's never mentioned him. If Bob hadn't heard about it from a mutual friend, I doubt we'd have a clue."

"The brothers don't get along?"

"The Sphinx doesn't say."

"Sphinx. It suits him. He ever lighten up?"

"There's more to him than anybody understands, I'm convinced. Alex's smart and knows his stuff. Got instincts that won't quit. Nobody bets against his hunches."

"Feebs are jerks, anyway. Don't want to get their hands dirty with the real work."

"Alex's not like that. He doesn't sneer at local cops." He

lifted a shoulder. "Just go slow and show him you're not a hot dog. That's the one thing he hates worse than anything. He's a hardass if he thinks you're taking stupid chances. But otherwise, he's great." He eyeballed the stairs ahead. "So—ready to race me?"

With a lightness she didn't feel, she answered the challenge. "Why not?"

"Ready, set—" He charged up three steps before saying "Go."

"Cheater!" she shouted. His good humor was hard to resist.

She'd already had quite a workout this morning, and six floors were tougher when you were laughing. They burst through the doorway and leaned against the wall, chuckling in between gasps for air.

Alex heard the door fly open. Then he heard the laughter, one voice obviously Sean's, the other feminine but low. Sultry.

He looked out into the hall. Sean was bent over, hands resting on his knees, his shoulders shaking with laughter.

But Jade was the one he couldn't quit staring at, and that was a problem.

Too many memories from early this morning roared through his brain. Alex shoved them away and leaned against the doorway with a casualness he didn't feel. "Having fun?"

She jumped as though she'd been hit with a cattle prod, the laughter vanishing in an instant. Sean straightened more slowly, his gray eyes not the least apologetic.

"Hey, Alex. Found us a kindred soul. She likes to take stairs. Not much competition for you or me, but maybe she can beat Bob—"

She jammed an elbow in his side, and Sean danced away, chuckling.

"He cheated, sir." Traces of laughter still glittered in her eyes, and Alex found himself sorry he wasn't the one who'd put them there.

"When you two get through clowning around, you might want to try reading the case files that just showed up from APD. That is, if you can spare time from field day. We'll meet in an hour to talk tactics."

Her back went ramrod straight, all humor gone from her face. "Yes, sir." The careful, cool woman was firmly in place. She headed for the cubbyhole she'd been assigned, and Alex saw one hand tighten into a fist.

He glanced at Sean and noted his curious stare. Alex cocked one eyebrow. "You waiting for an engraved invitation?"

Sean shook his head. "Uh-uh. Just enjoying watching you ride somebody else for a change." He gave Alex a cocky grin.

"Get out of here before I remember why Doc needs to bust you back to patrol."

"Sure thing, *sir*." He sketched an exaggerated salute, then walked away, whistling.

At the meeting, Jade looked around the table, enjoying the usual cop BS and shop talk while quizzing herself on the names. Ben Capwell was on loan from APD Homicide as liaison for this case. Evan Forbes was Department of Public Safety; Charlie Sampson, a Travis County deputy. APD Sgt. Marco de la Garza she already knew. Case Maxwell, Asst. U.

S. Attorney, was there to provide guidance on what would be needed to indict. With Sean, Bob and herself, that was the team.

Sandoval walked in, and everyone immediately fell silent. She couldn't bring herself to call him Alex yet. He had about him a natural air of command. A born leader, even among this group of the best and the brightest.

"All right. Let's talk tactics. We'll concentrate first on the clubs where these girls were last seen. Everyone but Butler goes out canvassing this afternoon, speaking to bartenders, bouncers, you name it. Catch them before the rush hits, so they've got time to talk.

"Butler, I don't want you in the bars until we're ready to bait the trap. You review the club video and the background info on these girls. Go over the interviews with the friends who saw them last. You're closer to their ages. Maybe you'll pick up on something no one else noticed."

She noted that he, too, was uncomfortable using first names between them. Maybe it was just the caution necessary in today's workplace to avoid any hint of sexual overtones— then again, he'd made his distaste for her involvement clear.

Jade counseled herself not to get bent out of shape that she was being held back from the main scene, aware that it was good management. No matter how eager she was to be an active part of this, her effectiveness would be compromised if she couldn't be kept out of the spotlight until they went live. She had a role to play and the stage wasn't set yet. They couldn't know if someone who worked at one of these establishments was involved with the disappearances.

"Those of you hitting the clubs head on out. Butler, you come to my office and—"

Bob appeared in the doorway. "Sorry to interrupt, but I think your plans just changed," he said. "One of the girls has turned up in the southeast part of town. Dead." His face hardened. "According to the patrol unit on the scene, looks like we got a weirdo on our hands."

Sandoval's eyes shot first to her as if her reaction were somehow important.

She gave him none.

He scanned the room. "All right, everybody. Let's go see."

Faces grim, they rose and filed out. She was almost out the door when he spoke again. "Butler, you ride with me."

Startled, she tried hard not to show it. Glances slid her way, and her temper stirred. Sean grinned and lifted one eyebrow. It was all she could manage to bite back the hasty words hovering on her tongue.

But she managed. She'd do whatever was required to prove herself to him.

One good thing, however. She was getting accustomed to hearing his voice. It was losing its power to shake her. He was just a man. An ordinary man. He *had* saved her life, but he wasn't superhuman. Barely human at times—to her, anyway. He'd rudely walked out on her in the gym.

None of that mattered now. As ordered, she followed him to his vehicle, a black SUV.

He glanced across the hood at her. The wolf-yellow eyes were hard as agate. Beautiful, but forbidding.

"You got a problem, Butler?"

"No, sir." She emphasized the *sir* and forced herself to meet his gaze evenly. She waited until he broke the connection before lowering herself into the seat.

The blocks flew past as they traveled in a silence that was almost a living thing, crackling and edgy.

At the scene, he stopped the car and shut off the engine, then studied her. Finally, he spoke. "From the sound of it, this one might be tough."

She shrugged. "I'll handle it."

His skepticism fairly shouted, but at last he broke the gaze. "Let's go."

The patrol units were right, Alex concurred a couple of minutes later. Whoever had done this was twisted.

Despite all the crime scenes he'd visited, the pervasive evidence he'd witnessed of man's inhumanity to man, he never quite got over wishing he could shield the dead from the eyes of the curious. Even in this warehouse on the outskirts of Austin where everyone here was only doing his job, there was still the impact when death was violent, the first shock you hoped you never totally lost.

If you did, you needed to leave the job because you'd forfeited the last shred of your own humanity.

He peered at Jade, to see how she was taking it. Her face was composed, her posture straight. But you could see her reaction in her hands, those graceful fingers that tightened with the emotion she wouldn't let her face show.

The girl had been arranged with care, bound to a chair naked, her long blond hair draping her face. In the shadows, Alex was almost certain he saw bruises. Her upper chest trailed blood from multiple crisscross slashes. Around her neck were wrapped strands of something plastic—celluloid film, he realized upon drawing closer. Hundreds more strands wrapped her body.

"What the hell—?" Sean muttered.

"Cause of death?" Alex asked the medical examiner.

"Soon as the photo techs are ready, we'll unwrap her hair.

Some of the wounds are premortem, but they didn't bleed enough to be the sole cause. I'll lay odds we'll find ligature marks on her throat."

"Her face is battered," Alex noted. "Normally, I'd say this guy falls into the organized class, but at some point, he lost his temper with her. She wasn't killed here, though."

"True," the ME responded.

Alex walked slowly around the perimeter, past where the forensics technicians were working. He glanced up once and thought he saw Jade's lips move, but no sound emerged. She was pale, but not inordinately so. He always watched new team members, even though their supervisors had vetted them.

And God knows, compared with the bloodbath she'd endured, this scene was mild.

Even as he was thinking about Jade, he was already building a profile of this case in his mind, and what he was coming up with was anything but reassuring. Rituals, fetishes, props—they were dealing with more than girls who hadn't bothered to call home.

The rage was a disturbing element. Disorganized killers lost their tempers, but their victims were abandoned where the act occurred, often in plain sight, not transported and artfully displayed. This man had planned ahead, gathered props, found both the place where he'd have all the time he wanted to kill the girl and a spot to leave her when he was finished.

And his neighbors probably would tell you he was the soul of kindness. He was clever and he'd never draw attention. He could keep this up for months.

Alex cast another look at Jade, who'd already seen more than anyone should.

Who was ready to put herself in the path of a madman.

Whether or not he liked it, other girls would die if she didn't.

"Timetable just got moved up, folks. We hit the first club tonight."

He wanted more time to dig, to concoct a foolproof plan.

But the killer didn't care if they were ready.

So Alex would dog Jade's every step. He would protect her, as he'd failed to do before.

Chapter Three

A long, low whistle sliced through the air. Alex turned to pinpoint the source, but got distracted by the vision at the door.

Good God.

If he hadn't known to expect her, he'd never have believed it was the same woman. No more trim, tailored slacks or conservative blazers. No baggy gym clothes.

Jade Butler was dressed for a night on the town, and every man in the room had his tongue hanging out. Alex battled the urge to send her home right this second and make her change.

Sean recovered first. "Holy smokes, Jade. Where'd you hide that figure?"

Pinpoints of color rose in her cheeks, and for a second, she froze. Then she drew herself up straight and swung that godforsaken russet hair, unbound and rippling almost to her waist.

"Very funny, Sean. Where's the tech?"

The tech was trying to un-swallow his tongue like the rest of them. Tight through the bodice and halfway down her hips, flaring into a skirt that flirted with her thighs, the short red dress barely qualified for the name. Tiny straps appeared underqualified to handle the curves beneath.

Jade Butler had been born in the wrong decade. She was a

throwback, in this age of boyish hips, to a fifties screen goddess.

The tech cleared his throat. "I don't see where I'm going to attach the unit."

"Here—I brought a purse that does the trick." Her eyes sparked as she held out her hand. "If you're all through making asses of yourselves, I'm ready to work."

Everyone got suddenly busy with something else.

Except Alex. "I told you I don't like cowboys, Butler."

She met his glare. "Neon grabs attention faster than crayons on poster board, wouldn't you agree?"

"That dress is beyond neon," Sean murmured. "Speaking as your new big brother, I'm sticking to you like glue."

"No, you're not," she warned. "Or he won't get within a mile of me."

"We're all going to be breathing down your neck, so get used to it," Alex ordered. "No woman clothed like that is going to be standing alone for long. Doesn't mean the scenery can't change."

"I know my job, *sir*." She plucked the apparatus from the tech's hand and spun away.

He watched the skirt sway gently against long, long legs lifted to a killer curve by what appeared to be four-inch heels.

"All right, people," he snapped. "Let's get cracking. It's showtime."

And you're on a very short leash, Jade Butler.

Hours later, Jade was dead on her feet. She'd talked, she'd smiled, she'd nursed drinks, she'd danced—and all she had to show for it was a pounding headache and toes that screamed.

Sean crossed her field of vision and gave a quick nod toward the door.

Hallelujah. Time to roll up the show and move on. This bar, where the dead girl had had her last fling, was not going to give up any secrets this evening.

Jade ducked past a brewing fight and around a group of women figuring the last cent of a bill, careful to maintain the pretense that she could still dance all night.

Outside Wild Child, a gleaming black Corvette, one of the cool cars the FBI had provided, pulled up. One of the benefits of the Feebs bankrolling VICTAF was access to vehicles confiscated from drug dealers under federal racketeering statutes. Jerks the Bureau boys might be, but they had great toys.

Bob grinned from behind the wheel. "Long night?"

She kicked off the ice-pick heels and rubbed her feet. "Women are idiots. Must have been a guy who convinced them heels like this look sexy."

"We're evil and disgusting. Pity us all."

She chuckled and let her head fall back, yawning. "I could sleep for a week."

"Catch a few winks. Traffic's tied up on the interstate and backing up to the access road, so I have to wind around to get back to the office."

"Nah—I'm fine." But she was tempted. She'd suddenly lost every ounce of the manic energy that had propelled her through the night.

The tension of the past couple of days caught up with her. As she felt the tight spring inside her unwinding, Jade struggled, realizing she should stay focused, think about her report—

Maybe, just for a minute, though, it would be okay to relax. She leaned her head on one fist, curled her legs beneath her. Breathed a long, slow sigh. She'd close her eyes for a second, then…

The murmur of male voices penetrated slowly. Jade stirred, drawing in an unfamiliar, alluring scent. Woodsy with a touch of spice and something she couldn't define. She rubbed her nose with one finger and resisted waking.

"Butler?" A deep voice prompted.

"Mmm?" She tried to blink, but her lids weighed a ton.

"Butler, wake up."

She jolted and blinked.

Golden-brown eyes studied her with a fleeting trace of warmth. As she fought her way through the fog, she heard low chuckles at her back. She whipped her head around and saw Sean and Bob.

Jade scrambled out of the car and lost her balance.

"Whoa, Detective. Easy—" Sandoval's hands closed around her waist to steady her.

The warmth of his touch unnerved her more. "I—I'm sorry. I don't know what—"

She stepped on a pebble and stifled a yelp. Oh, man. Fully aware now, she realized that she'd fallen asleep. Hadn't sensed the car stopping. How long had the team been standing there?

She whirled away.

He walked up beside her, his broad shoulders blocking the others. He held out her red high heels. "Don't sweat it. You were tired."

She couldn't look at him. Any of them. She straightened her shoulders, took her shoes. Reached with shaky fingers for her poise. "I apologize, sir." She forced her voice to steady.

"It shouldn't have happened."

"It was a long night, and you worked hard. You want a ride home?"

"No." God, no. She lifted her chin and forced herself to face the assembled group. "I'm fine. I'll be in early," she said, holding herself stiffly.

"Not necessary, Detective. We'll have another late one tomorrow." His voice had gone neutral. "Meeting at eleven, everyone. Get some rack time—you're going to need it."

With relief, she noted no smirks, only nods and quiet goodbyes. They all seemed exhausted.

Even the Sphinx.

Regardless, Jade couldn't get out of there fast enough.

To follow her home was reckless; nevertheless, he felt responsible. She was groggy. He'd do the same for any member of the team.

But it was harder every day to remember the coltish fifteen-year-old he'd carried around in his mind all these years. The grown Jade kept blurring the image. Beautiful, though she tried to hide it. Strong and capable.

Focus on that, Sandoval. She's a good cop. Step away and let her do her job. Treat her like any other team member. You've never had trouble working with women before.

Just one of the guys.

Alex snorted, shaking his head. Yeah, right.

But he'd do it, damn it. They were almost to her house. He'd stand guard until she got inside the door.

Alex pulled to a stop and watched her alight from the car, his foot jiggling impatiently on the brake. *Come on, Jade, what's*

the holdup? Go ahead so I can leave—

Then, through the dappled streetlight's glow, he caught a glimpse of her face. Desolation, coupled with loneliness.

And suddenly, the two faces merged again. Strong, grown up Jade resembled too much the younger version whose world had shattered. Shoulders bowed, she slipped inside.

Alex slammed the car into Park and emerged.

He owed her. He always would. He'd deserted that girl when she'd asked only to meet the man who'd been her lifeline, the person she called a hero.

That man hadn't been able to face his failure to save her from more horror than any young girl should ever see.

Though he'd rather take a bullet than discuss that night, he wouldn't walk away again. He could handle this. He'd simply talk to her for a minute, make sure she was okay, then he'd leave. Just for tonight, she looked as if she could use a friend.

Jade closed the door and leaned back against it, wondering if she could make the trip to her bedroom without falling, even as she dredged for the energy to let her dog, Major, inside for the night.

What was wrong with her? Yes, the evening had been a long one, but she'd had worse. Sure, she was tired and not sleeping well, but she'd long ago learned to live with erratic sleep.

The problem was Alex. Why did that body, that man, have to house the voice she'd idolized? He stood in her way; he was complicated. He stirred up too much inside her. Then, just when she thought she'd figured out how to deal with him, he had to go be nice to her.

The knock on the wood behind her back triggered automatic instincts. She drew her weapon from her purse, then peered through the peephole in the door.

When she saw who it was, she dropped her head and swore. With one hand, she jerked open the door. "Yes?"

His concerned gaze went immediately to her weapon, then swept up to her face. "I wanted to be sure you made it home all right."

"I told you I could handle it. Good night."

He grabbed the door before she could shove it closed. "Something's bothering you."

Jade turned away. "I'm fine. Leave—please." Begging stuck in her craw.

"Jade, how long are we going to dance around this?"

Everything inside her froze solid. "Around what?" She kept her back to him.

He swore softly. Behind her, she heard him step into the room.

"Don't—" She whirled, hoping to forestall him. *Get rid of him, get him away—*

But he was right there in front of her. Too big, too strong, too—

Male.

She'd all but buried the part of her that was female, afraid that her mother's weakness ran within. So far in her life, it hadn't been much of a struggle.

Until now.

Desperation seized her. "I asked you to go."

His stone mask slipped. Across it she saw emotions she couldn't quite pinpoint. Anger, yes, but also something…haunted.

"No one knows, do they?"

Her heartbeat sounded unnaturally loud inside her ears. "What are you talking—"

He didn't give her a chance to demur. "Stop stalling, Jade. That night…" His voice trailed off, but his eyes blazed with turmoil. "We never met, but you realize who I am, don't you?"

"The Voice," she murmured.

His eyes widened. "What?"

She glanced down at the floor. "In my mind, I always called you The Voice. I never knew your name."

A faint smile ghosted across his lips, but his eyes weren't amused. "Why on earth are you doing police work? I'd think it would be the last option you'd want to consider. Doesn't it bring that night back?"

"Sometimes." She shrugged one shoulder. "I wanted to be a person who protected others, who rescued them. Someone like you."

"What?" Shock reverberated through his tone. "Why the hell would you say that?"

Jade frowned. "You saved my life. You were a hero."

Fury, not pleasure, roared into his expression. "Your mother was murdered right before your eyes."

"But I wasn't, thanks to you."

"You don't know what you're talking about. You went through a nightmare." He grabbed her shoulders and shook her, then just as suddenly released her. Stepped back.

"So why didn't you come when I asked for you? I wanted to thank the man who rescued me."

Agitation rippled through his powerful frame. "Stop it. You have no idea—" He shoved his fingers through his hair. "You were just a kid. Hell, you're still a kid," he muttered.

Answering fury rose. "I'm a grown woman and a damn good cop."

His rage stung the air around them. "What if you get in a hostage situation again? How will you react?"

"How will *you?*" she retorted.

Grief crossed his face, and she regretted her temper. "I'm sorry. I shouldn't have asked that."

He waved off the apology. "No, you're right. Everyone has baggage. A past. The good cops don't let it interfere."

"I never have. I am a good cop. Ask anyone." She held her breath.

A curt nod. "I already checked you out. If I didn't believe that, you wouldn't be on the team."

Relief rushed through her like a cooling wind. "Thank you."

"Show your gratitude by staying one. If I see the first sign of that night affecting your performance, I'm telling Doc."

She couldn't let him do that. "You have no right to hold it against me. I was the victim of a crime, not the perpetrator. You try to use it to get me out of VICTAF, and I'll file discrimination charges against you."

He stared at her, eyes hard.

She jutted her chin.

Then, to her shock, his mouth curved in a faint grin. "You had moxie even then, kid."

"I'm not a kid," she reminded him.

His gaze scanned her from head to toe. She felt exposed in the red dress in a way she hadn't all night.

"I know." His eyes flared hot for an instant so brief she might have imagined it. "Go to bed, Detective." In his rough voice one tender note slid against her hearing like velvet against her skin. Then he walked to the door.

For a moment, she wished again to be held in those strong arms—but this time, it was a woman, not a child who did the wishing.

"Alex—"

He stopped at the door, his broad shoulders stiffening. "What?" He didn't turn around.

The temptation to ask for comfort was strong. Ruthlessly, she strangled it. "Thank you."

He stilled for a second.

Then, without a word, he left.

Jade remained motionless long after the sound of his car died away.

With a shiver, she broke from her trance. *Bed, Jade. Rest. You've never needed a clear head more.*

The phone rang. Barechested, clad only in paint-smeared jeans, Alex considered ignoring it.

Then he swore beneath his breath. This canvas would have to be trashed, anyway. Power sometimes resulted from his unleashed emotions, but not tonight. What he'd painted was crap.

And calls at six a.m. weren't meant to be ignored.

After grabbing a rag to wipe his hands, Alex made it to the phone on the fourth ring. "Yeah?"

"I thought you'd be up." His older brother Rafe. "Sorry to call you this early, but I knew you'd be gone for your workout if I waited too long."

"What's up? Everyone okay back there?" It was an hour earlier in their West Texas hometown of La Paloma.

"Yeah." Then he snickered. "Well, Liam might not say quite that. Sexiest Man Alive is a little cranky these days."

"Baby still not sleeping through the night?"

"Apparently, Liam's daughter is a nocturnal creature. She

takes long naps and hits the sack right after dinner, but just about the time Raina and Liam are falling asleep, she comes alive and is good to go for hours yet. To little brother's credit, since Raina is the only one who can nurse Gracie, he takes her after and gives Raina a chance to rest."

Alex chuckled. "I bet Mom is enjoying this. The son who would never go to bed before three a.m. is getting his come-uppance."

"She's smirked a few times."

Alex couldn't yet picture his youngest brother as a dad, though he'd gone home for a quick visit as soon as he'd heard that Raina was in labor. He'd seen Liam absolutely beaming over his tiny daughter, now six months old, but he hadn't been able to make it back since the birth, though he got frequent reports and pictures emailed to him. Grace Celeste Sullivan had captured the hearts of the whole family from the first second she'd drawn breath.

"I miss you guys," Alex blurted. He hadn't realized how he'd needed this dose of normalcy.

"Not for long, you won't."

"What do you mean?"

"Diana and I are heading back to Dallas soon, and Dad and Mom want to come to Austin, so they can see you and visit Jilly when she returns from spring break. He thinks you should get up a poker game at your place while they're here. Have some guy time to cuss and smoke cigars."

Something inside Alex relaxed at the thought of his step-father. Hal Sullivan was their mother's second husband, father to Dane and Liam and Jilly. He was nothing like their late, beloved father, Roberto Sandoval, but both Rafe and Alex knew how lucky they'd been that their mother, Celeste, had found him. A big man always ready with a hearty laugh, he'd never tried to take their father's place or make them feel anything but proud of their Latino heritage. Celeste would never have stood for it, anyway—she'd refused to go home to her family when widowed, instead making sure he and Rafe could remain close to their paternal grandmother, whom they called Abuelita, and the tiny village of La Paloma where they had been born and raised.

Hal had stood behind them every step of adolescence, teaching them both, by example, what a man was and did. Their paths had been more complicated, being of mixed heritage, but what Hal lacked in experience with their culture, he amply made up for in fierce devotion and strong protective instincts. Roberto had been Papa, but Hal was Dad in more than just the name.

"I'll get the cards ready and stock the refrigerator with beer."

"Great. Now, tell me what's wrong."

Once a big brother, always a big brother, though their roles had been reversed for a time when Rafe was struggling first to survive, then to walk again, after his Special Forces team was ambushed. "Nothing," Alex said.

"Yeah, I'm buying that. Bad case?"

"A nasty one. Three girls missing, one turned up dead yesterday with all the marks of a ritual slaying."

"Damn. I was hoping things would be quieter once you left D.C. Austin's not prone to that sort of thing."

"Not usually, but bad guys don't respect city limits signs."

"You said the task force is stacked with solid cops. You have a good team on this case?"

"Yeah, except for one—" *Not fair, Alex. She's good. You just don't*—He realized he'd missed what his brother had said. "What?"

"I imagine you'll fix the problem pretty quick. You don't tolerate slack performance."

"She's not slacking. She's just—"

"Ah." Rafe chuckled. "*She.* Now I get it."

Though there was sympathy in Rafe's voice, Alex bristled. "No. You don't."

Rafe went silent, and Alex berated himself for bringing his unease into the respite of talking to his brother. "Sorry—it's just that—"

"No. I'm the one who should apologize. This isn't simple woman trouble, is it?"

At the moment, Alex rued the very skills that made his brother such a powerful healer. Just like Abuelita, Rafe always seemed to see beneath the surface. They weren't even in the same room—were six hundred miles apart, in fact—and his brother still understood too much.

His shoulders sagged. "I don't know what it is." The sleepless night pulled at him, dragged him under. "Listen, I have to go. This case—"

"If the timing's bad for them to visit—"

"No." He'd been far away by choice for years now, but the draw of his family had begun to wear at his solitude. He knew that they'd allowed him space to create his life, but they'd never given up on luring him back to the fold.

He'd always loved his family; he'd just needed to find his own way. Now he was ready to come home. He'd wanted to be a cop since he was a little kid, but the job was hell on relationships, especially romantic ones. Aside from one two-year stint with a fellow agent, Alex's love life had been safely restricted to women who had no interest in permanence.

But a part of him was tired of standing outside the window looking in while other people lived, loved, laughed…took the simple joys of existence for granted because someone else guarded them from the dark, seamy underbelly.

"I want to see them. You, too, if you can come down to

Austin at some point. I can't tell where things will be with this investigation by then, but—"

"You'll do what you can, and Dad and Mom will live with it," Rafe said. "And you know I'm here when you're ready to talk, right?"

He'd shut himself off from too much. Not completely—they wouldn't stand for it, any of them. Some part of his family was always checking in with him, making sure he understood without the words having to be said that he was never alone, no matter how much time passed between visits.

And this family member was the closest of all. Two years apart, they'd weathered their father's death together, backed each other in teenage fights, engaged in stupid stunts...out of a tight-knit family, no bond was stronger than the one he had with the man on the other end of the phone.

"Yeah," he answered. "I do." He smiled. "Take care of that woman of yours, brother. She's solid gold."

"More than I deserve," Rafe said, his voice echoing with love.

"No, she's not." If anyone on this earth had earned happiness, it was Rafe. He'd paid a heavy price for it, even before he'd chosen to devote his life to caring for those the world passed by.

"Well." Rafe cleared his throat. "See you soon, bro."

"Will do. Give Abuelita a hug for me."

"She'd prefer one in person, however, I'll do that. Be careful, Alex."

"Always am." Alex disconnected, but didn't set the phone down just yet.

Chapter Four

The alarm screamed in her ear. Jade groped on the bedside table and knocked the clock to the floor. When she finally succeeding in silencing it, she sank against the bed, tempted to slide face down and grab a few more Zs. She blinked at the dial. Six-thirty. With a groan, she realized she'd forgotten to reset the alarm.

Crawling back under the covers, she heard Major's whimper. Two seconds later, a tongue slicked up her cheek and a wet nose sniffed at her hair. Doggy breath wafted into her nostrils.

She cocked one eye open. "My meeting isn't until eleven." How sad was it, to be reduced to pleading with a dog?

Part cocker spaniel, part border collie, Major wagged his tail and let his tongue hang out of a cheery dog grin. He leaned forward to bestow another canine kiss.

Jade jerked to sitting. "Okay, okay…I'm up." She scrubbed her face with one hand as she ruffled his black fur with the other. Major wagged his tail in delight for a second, then whipped away toward the bedroom door, whimpering again.

"Doggy door," Jade muttered. They weren't that secure, but it would be the first thing she did when she owned her own home. Her savings were growing, if far too slowly, but she was on target for the next stage of her plan. Except for the years with her grandparents, Jade had been a tenant all her life—and even with them, she'd felt no more settled, aware that she was only there on sufferance. Her grandparents had considered it their Christian obligation to take in the bastard child of their wayward daughter, but dry duty was all she'd had from them.

She would give her own children more. Much more.

If she ever found someone with whom she wanted to have them. Many women had to be single mothers, but Jade would not be one of them, not intentionally. She would not bring children into the world unless she found that one right man with whom to raise them.

She freed Major to race outside and sank to the steps, stretching the football jersey to cover goose-pimpled legs. Joyfully, Major chased the blue jays that had had the nerve to settle on his fence, pausing only seconds to relieve his full bladder before patrolling his territory, marking every few feet with fierce, determined progress.

Jade had achieved one dream—to be a cop—but she had others. A home of her own, filled to the rafters with family, was no less important. Maybe more so. She'd cherished that one long before the hostage experience that had sent her in search of justice.

She went inside and opened the freezer to retrieve coffee beans, before remembering that she was out. Trey, her favorite coffee shop proprietor, had reminded her two days ago that she was likely running low. She'd scoffed, and he'd shrugged with his usual cheer.

He'd been right, damn it. Now she'd have to stop in and eat crow.

Her shower was long and hot as she worked out the soreness in her calves from those blasted heels. Tonight she'd go more casual. Two in a row in those killer shoes would leave her crippled for life.

Recalling last night brought with it thoughts of the man who'd followed her home, and Jade scowled. She didn't know what to make of him, and uncertainty was a force she'd worked to banish from her life.

How long are we going to dance around this?

There was nothing more to discuss. She'd made of herself someone as different from that child, tossed around by fate, as possible. No one, not even Alex Sandoval, could be allowed to force her back.

As she moved to her room to dress, her gaze caught on the basket of fabric scraps she was attempting to piece into a quilt. Her fellow cops would laugh if they could see her efforts to learn the art of feathering a nest, but the home she would one day create would have everything of security and comfort, nothing of the temporary she'd had with Belle or the starkness and sterility she'd endured with her grandparents.

She had no examples to follow, but that was nothing new. Her whole life was crafted of scraps harvested from glimpses of what normal life should be.

She glanced around her at the discarded furniture she'd scavenged and refurbished. She had a strict budget, and home ownership came first, but something in her hungered for beauty. She'd learned to haunt thrift shops and garage sales. Sandpaper and paint and elbow grease could turn trash to treasure if you just had patience and weren't afraid of hard work.

She'd been her own biggest project. Alex Sandoval would learn soon enough the power of her determination and will.

With haste, she finished dressing, the pleasant reverie of her dreams of family and home evaporated by thoughts of the harsh man who so confused her. He was nothing like the hero she'd dreamed; so be it. That made things easier, actually. She'd quit trying to make him into something he wasn't and focus on proving to him who she was now.

Not the traumatized girl who'd clung to his comfort.

After feeding and watering Major and roughhousing with him for a few pleasure-filled minutes, she gave him the daily chew bone and headed out the door to begin the process by beating the Sphinx to the office.

Don't bet against me, Alex Sandoval. You're not the toughest hurdle I've had to vault. Her smile was grim as she started her car.

She shouldn't have been surprised to find herself not the first one to arrive at the office. Doc was already in, as was Bob.

Sandoval, too, though he granted her only the faintest of acknowledgments.

She gave him none.

Cop coffee in hand, already sorry she hadn't stopped for the Trey's far superior brew, Jade sat down at her desk and pulled up the interviews she'd read yesterday, focusing on the friends of DeDe Fairchild, the girl who was no longer missing. She hit keys to display her picture on the screen, alive, eyes sparkling in the sorority photo.

The contrast to the body Jade had viewed could be no more striking. So young the girl in the photo was. So confident that she'd be more than a match for whatever life would hand her.

Why? Jade asked silently. *Why did you go with him? What did he promise you?*

What does a killer have to offer that a girl like you, beautiful and moneyed, doesn't already possess?

She cast her mind back over the scene, eyes squeezed shut as she saw past the pretty face, imagined the skin unmarked, unbloodied…intact and perfect, the figure smooth and curvy—

Her eyes popped open. Quickly she scanned the lab reports to determine the origin of the film coiled around the girl's body like an obscene gift wrapping.

Movie film, just as they'd guessed. Had the lab checked to see if there were relevant images on it? She scrolled down the screen, but saw no notes to indicate either way.

That could be it, though. Fame. It was what their killer could offer that DeDe Fairchild, sorority girl with everything, couldn't grant herself.

Jade decided to call the lab. If she was right, she had an idea of what to look for when she cruised tonight—someone posing as a photographer or director. Austin was lousy with wannabe filmmakers. UT had one of the top film departments in the country.

And one component of South by Southwest was a film festival.

She shot to her feet, head swiveling for someone to ask, to share this idea with—

Sean walked in the door. When he caught sight of her, he grinned and swerved toward her cubicle. "You're awfully bright eyed this morning. I thought you'd be—" He shook his head. "Sorry. I didn't mean—"

Her euphoria dissipated as she remembered how she'd embarrassed herself in front of the team last night.

She sat back down. "Forget it."

He leaned against her desk. "I can't. I was out of line. You were tired, that's all."

She snorted, focused on the screen. "Everyone was tired, Sean, but I fell asleep."

He settled one hip on the desk and leaned into her field of vision. "The rest of us weren't center stage or wearing four-inch heels." Then he grinned. "Damn, but you've got some legs on you, Jade."

She started to retort, then realized he was yanking her chain. His expression was anything but repentant. "Jerk," she responded, relaxing as she understood that he was on her side. "How much grief am I going to have to take over that?"

"A lot." His smile widened. "Want me to protect you from the mean men?"

"Oh yeah. That'll help." She scrubbed hands over her face. "I want a do-over."

"Take your medicine like a man, Jade."

She exhaled in a gust. "Always have. I should be used to the obstacle course by now."

"You could cry. Girls know guys can't take tears."

"Shut up, Sean I'm a cop, not a girl."

"I beg to differ. First night off we get, I'll be glad to demonstrate the finer points of the male-female difference. Not because I want to, you understand. Only because my mama raised me right."

"In an alternate universe." She shoved at his hip. "Get off my desk and let me work." He complied, still chuckling. Then she remembered. "Wait—there's a film component to South by Southwest."

His forehead wrinkled. "Yeah."

"What are the dates this year?"

"The South by Southwest Film Festival starts three days before the music festival," came a voice from behind her. "Why?"

"Hey, Alex," Sean greeted.

Jade didn't want to turn around, but she would allow no cowardice in herself. To gain advantage, she rose from her chair before facing him. "Has the lab checked the film wrapped around the victim yet to see what's on it?"

"What does the file say?"

"Nothing reported yet. I'd like to ask them to do so if they haven't." She paused. "*Sir*," she added for effect.

His frown deepened. "No *sirs* needed. In case you weren't listening to Doc, we're all equals here, Butler."

Some of us more equal than others. But she didn't say it.

"What are you thinking?" he asked.

She didn't allow herself to hesitate, though she wasn't eager to risk more embarrassment. "In reviewing the data, I realized that this girl led a charmed life—moneyed background, attractiveness, all the advantages. I tried to imagine what anyone would have to offer that she couldn't get on her own—what would make her leave a bar with a stranger."

One eyebrow cocked. "We don't know that it was a stranger."

Her jaw tightened, but she persisted. "We aren't sure of much yet, *Agent Sandoval*." She felt satisfaction at the displeasure that crossed his features as she emphasized their relative positions. Though he hadn't pulled rank on her, she was edgy enough not to care this morning. "It's as valid to assume it was a stranger as not, and if so, I need to know what to be looking for tonight."

She breezed on. "She's a very pretty girl, but the university's full of them. She probably got used to being the beauty of her high school, and now all of a sudden, she's only one of thousands." Jade paused, thinking of the girl named Most Beautiful in the small Oklahoma high school she'd suffered through on her way out. "Some girls, that's all they are, their looks. They grow up being treated special simply because they're easy on the eyes."

She's beautiful, Alex thought, *but she doesn't know it.* Jade never saw that reaction from people, he realized. Not because they didn't give it but because she'd always been too busy trying to survive her life.

What had those years been like? he wondered. After she'd been swept away into the bosom of family, why hadn't she noticed her beauty reflected in the eyes of others?

And when his nightmares had been so full of her, why hadn't he checked?

Because during your waking hours, you were too busy burying that night.

"So what's your point?" he said abruptly.

Sean frowned at him. Alex was only too aware of his short temper after not enough sleep. Of what had passed between him and Jade the night before.

And years before.

She wasn't cowed, though. Her eyes simmered. "Fame," she responded. "Austin's full of photographers and filmmakers, both amateur and pro. Maybe he offered her a chance to rise out of the ranks of pretty girls and become a star."

A good angle. "What about the other two girls?"

Her jaw tightened. "I was just about to review their files."

He nodded. "Do it. If they were attractive, too, look for high school acting experience, modeling, drill team, anything that indicates—"

"Ambition," she interrupted. "Vanity."

She's good, he thought. Deserves to hear it. "It's a smart angle." He tried to ignore the glow that lit her face, but didn't succeed. "We're running everything through the DPS lab—call them and use my name. See if they've already examined the film, and if not, put a rush on it. Sean, contact UT's film department and also find out if there's a local film society. We need student rosters and membership lists. Transcripts for these girls, too."

"You got it." Sean headed for his desk.

Alex shot a glance at Jade, expecting triumph to be on her features. It was there, but so was confusion.

That makes two of us. He settled for a nod and left.

And pretended he didn't see her punch a fist into the air, jubilantly whispering *Yes!*

But he grinned to himself, knowing she'd earned it.

As the eleven o'clock meeting loomed, Jade's euphoria dimmed. One of the missing girls' profile could be stretched to resemble the dead girl's—she was pretty and had been a cheerleader, but she was a chemical engineering major with a solid 3.9 GPA, obviously more grounded in the life of the mind.

The other missing coed was of merely average looks and background. Her friends weren't even sure why she'd been in a bar, as it wasn't her usual style. Jade couldn't see anything about the girl that would fit her theory or why she would have drawn their man's notice.

She chewed on a pencil and stared at the screen as her stomach growled. The problem with not being a breakfast person.

"Mine's yelling, too. Want to grab a bite after the meeting?" Sean asked from behind her.

She bolted upright. "Stop sneaking up on me."

"I wasn't. You were too busy glaring at the computer. What's wrong?"

She threw the pencil on the desk and watched it bounce. He'd find out soon enough anyway. They all would. "My great idea won't wash."

"Why not?"

"One girl doesn't fit."

"How?"

Jade rubbed her forehead. "Average looks, shy. Friends say she doesn't do the bar scene." She checked her watch and rose. "Might as well give the Sphinx his chance to gloat."

"I don't think he will."

"Maybe." Sean didn't know Sandoval was hunting for an excuse to ditch her.

"Alex's hard but fair. Give him a chance, why don't you."

Tell him to give *me* a break, she thought. But didn't say it. "Sure thing."

Sean frowned. "What's the beef between you two?"

"Not one." She tried to slip past him into the doorway.

He halted her. "I asked around. No one indicated you were temperamental. Guys who've worked with you said you're too serious but you do good work. So what's got a burr up your butt about Alex?"

Before she could fire off a retort, a too-familiar voice spoke from inside the room.

"Would you two care to join the rest of us, or are we interrupting something more important?" Sandoval's tone made it clear that nothing carried more weight than the meeting they were delaying.

Jade glared at Sean as she slid beneath the arm he'd used to block her. "I'm not temperamental."

"Sure you're not," he fired back before he stalked around the table.

"Want to share that with the group, Sean?" Sandoval's look could have turned them both to stone.

"Nope." Sean dropped into the first open chair, forcing Jade to take the one closest to Sandoval.

"The kid's not used to rejection." Bob grinned to the accompaniment of chuckles. "Pretty Boy's usually fighting them off. Maybe I should study you, Sean. See if my technique needs some polish."

"First you gotta have technique, Bob." The laughter rose.

"Okay, people, down to business." Sandoval's voice brought them to immediate attention. "Bob, what's happening with the interviews of bar owners and employees?"

"We concentrated first on the place where the dead girl disappeared. Owner checks out clean. Not finished talking to all the employees present on the night in question, but so far most of them left at the expected time and can account for their whereabouts the rest of that night. Since the medical examiner believes the girl was killed three days later, there's a lot to investigate before we even get to the people on duty when the other two girls vanished."

"So no leads at all?"

"One bouncer, Rick Howard, cut out early. We haven't located him yet. He's a big guy and certainly has the physical strength to take her. No leads, though, on why she would have gone with him willingly, and no one recalls any sort of ruckus."

"He'd know the club well enough to sneak her out, though," Alex noted.

Bob nodded. "But no one remembers exactly when he left, relative to when she went missing. Club was just too busy that night, and the whole staff was hopping." He grimaced. "If they had video inside, we could answer both those questions pronto. We're checking into frequent patrons, too, hoping someone noticed something, but it's slow going."

"Stay after it," Alex urged. "Evan, you concentrate on the second bar and coordinate results with Bob. We've got to stop this guy before we find another one dead."

Then his dark eyes scanned the room, settling on her.

"Butler's got a theory we want to keep in mind as we compare notes."

"I don't—" she protested. "It's not going to work after all."

"Why not?"

"The last girl doesn't fit. Not in looks or motivation or background."

"She disappeared from the same bar as the first girl, so I'm not ready to rule out your theory. It's too early in the game for us to get invested in one angle. Just explain your idea to the rest of the group and tell us what you've discovered. Once everyone's reported, we'll see how things develop."

Instead of the humiliation she'd feared, she found support. Acknowledgment instead of pressure.

Maybe Sean was right about him being fair. She took a deep breath and began to talk.

Several minutes later, they'd gone around the room, placing their pieces of the puzzle on the table and examining them for a fit. Just as with a jigsaw, they assembled what they could of the edges of the frame and a few pieces scattered inside, but too much was still unknown.

Skillful and patient, Sandoval led them, handing out encouragement while urging greater effort, molding them into a cohesive unit. A team.

He was good. Very good. Sharp, yes, but more.

And for that span of time, she forgot their shared past, ignored his misgivings and her own and simply enjoyed matching wits with a group of dedicated officers of the law determined to find justice.

Until Sandoval asked Bob for the list of other female officers.

Her head swiveled toward him. "Why?"

He merely lifted one brow. "Your approval is not required for command decisions, Detective."

The room fell abruptly quiet. All eyes locked on her.

"If this is because of what I did last night—" She stopped, realizing he could take two meanings from it. She sure wasn't ready for the rest of them to know about his visit.

Dark brows snapped together. "You handled yourself competently, Butler. I'm merely keeping options open."

"Then why replace me?" The steel of her tone belied the quiver inside her.

"I haven't said I'll do that, but we may need more women undercover at some point. Your hair color makes you stand out. At the moment, that's an asset, but it might become a liability."

"I can change the color. I've done it before."

"Detective—" Warning laced his tone. "I need team players, not prima donnas."

"Prima—" She clamped her mouth shut. She couldn't let him get under her skin this way or she'd be out on her butt. "Yes, sir." Humiliation crowded her throat, right behind the fear. "It won't happen again."

His stare bored through her until she wanted to squirm. After an interminable lapse, his attention shifted to the group. "All of you have your assignments for the afternoon. Assemble here at seven-thirty for a final briefing before tonight's operation."

Chairs slid back as the team rose, their eyes skipping past Jade. She stood straight and forced herself to endure the covert scrutiny, her hands gripping the chair back. Only when the last of them had left, except for Sandoval, did she turn to go.

But he wasn't through with her.

"Butler." She could read nothing in his tone.

"Sir." She made herself face him, too.

"You asked me to give you a chance to prove yourself. This how you do it?"

She'd take each blow and remain standing. Damned if she wouldn't.

"I asked you a question. My place here is secure, but you can be back at APD before lunch."

"I'm aware of that, sir. I apologize." Every word was torn straight from her gut. "You want it in writing?"

His jaw hardened. His eyes smoldered. "Cut the formal crap, Jade. And can the *sir* bit. You're ticking me off, and I don't anger easily. Now, you explain to me why I should have any confidence in your abilities undercover when I can push your buttons with so little effort. You're supposed to be better than this."

"I am. It's just—" She snapped her mouth shut.

"Just what?"

"Nothing."

"Don't play cryptic, Jade. I'm better at it than you'll ever be. Explain yourself. Convince me why I should want you on this team."

"You don't—" Despite her intentions, her voice rose. "That's the problem. You've wished me off this operation since the second you laid eyes on me, and nothing I can say or do makes a difference. Is it that you doubt I can handle it if some guy grabs me? Even after I almost whipped your ass, you still wonder if I can defend myself?"

He didn't answer.

She persisted. "I don't need protecting. Just do your job, and I'll do mine. I'm not fifteen anymore."

A muscle leaped in his jaw. "I'm aware of that."

"No. You're not. And I deserve better." Jade spun on her heels and stalked out the door.

Chapter Five

Some days the bad guys looked tame compared with the press. Alex took the stairs two at a time to blow off steam after the press conference. Murders in D.C. had become so commonplace that even the media got blasé, but in Austin any murder was news, and a dead, pretty coed sent shivers down a lot of spines—politicians, administrators, parents of students…the list was long.

So far the details of the method hadn't leaked, but though the local media weren't as cannibalistic as their brethren on the national scene, they were also not so sanguine about violent death. And UT had, in addition to a top-notch film school, a journalism program that turned out a lot of hungry reporters.

At the top of the stairs, he hit the door primed and ready. They needed answers before another girl wound up dead.

Doc, who'd been in attendance at the press conference, met him in the hall. "Elevator's faster," he observed.

Alex only grunted.

"Handled yourself well with the media."

"They're just getting warmed up."

Bob approached. "Got the results on the film. Most of it's some kind of arty crap, but two frames are interesting. Photos are in your office."

"Ask Marco if he's got a minute to update me on the warehouse search," Alex said to the secretary. Inside his office, he snatched the sheets from his desk. "They're grainy."

"Lab said it had been filmed differently. No way to know if it was on purpose or lack of skill. They wouldn't even register on the eye at a showing."

She'd been right, he thought. The dead girl wore a costume in one. Naked in the other. Both shots seemed posed.

Alex swiveled, scanned the bullpen. "Where's Jade?"

"Court. Testifying."

Alex frowned at Doc. "I thought she was here full-time."

Doc held out his palms. "Prosecution said they had to have her testimony on this one."

"Which court? She needs to see these."

"District—my assistant can find out which one."

"Never mind. I've got a line on a homeless guy who's in jail right now. I'll check on her while I'm at the courts complex." He nodded at Bob. "Get the word out to meet an hour earlier."

"Sure thing."

He conferred with Marco de la Garza on the status of the canvass APD patrol units were conducting on empty warehouses. So far, no more dead girls, but his gut said their luck wouldn't hold.

A little while later, he slipped into the courtroom before Jade finished testifying. He grabbed a seat in the back and peered around an enormous head of hair.

"Detective, your surveillance unit malfunctioned rather conveniently, didn't it?" asked the defense attorney.

"You wouldn't say that if it was your skin getting scorched."

Laughter rippled through the room. Alex smiled.

"Nonetheless, as a result, it's your word against my client's that he tried to trap you in his car."

Jade didn't blink. "Unlike your client, I respect the law too much to lie."

"Don't you do exactly that every time you pose as something you're not? Isn't it a cruel hoax to take a young man from a desperate background and make him believe that you love him?"

"The defendant wouldn't accept no for an answer. No means no, whether it's a cop or a civilian. Your poor little client raped a girl, and he would have raped me if I hadn't been well-trained in self-defense."

"Self-defense or police brutality?" the defense lawyer asked.

"Objection, Your Honor." The prosecutor stood. "The officer is not on trial here. The record documents her injuries, whether or not the surveillance unit could back her up."

Injuries. Attempted rape. Yet she sat there, cool and composed, refusing to let the bad guys win.

She was right; he knew it. Even at fifteen, she'd handled herself well, kept her head.

She was grown now, and she didn't need him to stand between her and danger. His demons had to remain his own—she'd dealt with hers better than he had his, it seemed.

Alex settled back to watch her in action.

Jade's concentration had bobbled when he walked in, but she'd refocused quickly and studiously ignored him while sidestepping defense efforts to discredit her.

She'd done a damn good job, if she said so herself, but the toll of a restless night and the emotional scene earlier combined with the strain of dancing around sneaky lawyers to give her a killer headache.

When she emerged from the courtroom, all she wanted was half a bottle of aspirin, her missed lunch and forty winks, in that order.

Finding Alex Sandoval waiting did not make her wish list. She cut him a glance but kept walking.

He fell into step beside her. "You were good in there."

"Thanks. *"Now go away. I'm too tired to spar with you, too.*

He grabbed her arm, and she resisted until she realized he was helping her dodge the woman about to barrel into her.

"Thanks." She slid from his grasp as quickly as possible. "What are you doing here?"

He started to draw an envelope from his jacket, then frowned, staring at her. "You're exhausted."

She dodged his scrutiny. "I'm fine."

"Have you eaten?"

"I'll grab something later." *Unless my head explodes first.*

"Come here," he snapped. He took her elbow and led her down the stairs to the courthouse snack bar. "You've got a long night ahead. I can't afford for you to fade in the stretch."

She jerked from his grip. "I know my limits."

"Do you?" He simply used a hand at her back to steer her to the counter. "What do you want?"

"I don't—" Finally, she broke down and rubbed her temple. "Aspirin."

"None here, but food might help until we can get some."

"I'm not hungry." She was starving, but she wanted time alone worse.

"I am. I missed lunch, too." He scanned the counter. "Looks like our choices are ham and cheese or ham and cheese." He leaned to the left. "And some extremely yellow pudding," he said with a smile.

And what a smile it was, the first genuine one she'd seen from him. Despite everything, it took off some of the jagged edges of her day.

"What are you doing here?" she repeated.

"Got some pictures to show you."

"Of what?" Then she caught on. "The film. Where are they?"

"Right here." He tapped his breast pocket. "But first, we eat."

"Tell me what's in them."

Instead of answering, he nodded at the counter person. "Three ham and cheese, two packages of potato chips and—" He grinned. "You brave enough to dare the pudding?"

Okay, so he had charm, but he was stubborn. Still, short of wrestling him down, she wasn't getting the photos. Anyway, he'd lightened the mood. "That color yellow does not appear in nature."

Another quick, devastating smile. "Yeah. What do you want to drink?"

"What's got the most caffeine?" she queried the counter guy.

"Lack of energy is often due to poor hydration. Two large waters," he ordered.

"Thank you, Dr. Nutrition. Why did you bother asking me?"

He merely shrugged and pulled out his wallet.

"Oh, no, you don't. I pay my way."

"You can buy next time."

"Anybody ever tell you you're overbearing?"

"My family might have mentioned it a time or two." He pocketed the change and led her to a booth in the corner.

"How big is your family?"

"Don't you mean what's it like to have the Sexiest Man Alive as my brother?" But there was only fondness in his expression.

The two men looked nothing alike, but she thought the man before her was more compelling than his famous brother. "No. I mean, how many of you are there? Besides, having a movie star brother has to be a major pain in the behind."

Shadows moved in. "His fame comes with a stiff price. And Liam's a great guy."

"You love them." A statement, not a question.

"Yeah. I do."

"So?"

"So what?"

"How many?"

"One elder brother, Rafael. He's a *curandero*, married to a traditional doctor."

"What's a *curandero*?"

"An ancient healing tradition practiced in the Latino culture. Dates back to the Aztecs."

"You mean like witch…" Her voice trailed off.

"Witch doctors?" He grinned. "Faith healers?"

"Sorry. That sounded rude."

"Most Anglos have never heard of the tradition." His grin widened. "His wife, Diana, is a former cardiac surgeon. You think you're skeptical about it?" He shook his head. "Rafe was a Special Forces medic, but our grandmother is a *curandera*, and he's incorporating both traditions of medicine at the clinics for the indigent that he and Diana run in Dallas and the little town where he and I grew up near Alpine."

"He sounds interesting."

"He is." Alex finished off a sandwich. "He and I have the same father, who died when we were kids. Mom married Hal Sullivan, and they had three more—Dane, Liam and our brat sister, Jilly." Affection colored his tone.

"Where is she?"

"In school here at UT."

"No wonder you're so—"

His face turned solemn. "I'm not doing it for Jilly."

"Of course you are. Not solely for her, maybe, but you can't help but be worried."

"If I catch her on Sixth Street alone, I'll lock her in a convent for the rest of her life." His expression was grim. "I don't want to worry the family, and I can't compromise the case, but I'm going to talk to her when she gets back from spring break and ask her to stay away from the area until I clear it."

"Will she listen?"

"Jilly's impulsive, but she's smart." He passed one hand over his eyes. "Or maybe I'll just lock her up anyway."

His deep love for his family shone through every word. In sympathy, she touched the hand fisted on the table. "If she needs to hear it from someone besides an overprotective older brother, let me know."

"Thanks." He drew his hand back. "But I'm not overprotective. Just careful."

She could have argued; instead she let his assertion pass and finished her sandwich. "Okay, I ate. Now show me the photos."

"Drink your water."

"I'd rather throw it in your face."

"You'd get the photos wet."

They both chuckled.

He reached into his pocket, and Jade downed half of her water.

She accepted the envelope and used her body to shield the photos from view. She squinted, trying to make out the fuzzy shapes, then her eyes widened and she glanced up. "I was right," she marveled.

"Yeah." He nodded. "You were."

"Let's head back." She could probably fly, fueled by the euphoria.

His smile was warm and appreciative as he swept out an arm. "After you."

As Jade drove home three hours later, her head whirled with information. Dan Fleming, the DPS lab expert, had explained the film industry from the ground up, including the artistic integrity of film versus digital. He was a nice guy, patiently translating what he knew into layman's terms, giving her demonstrations on the lab's impressive equipment. Film projectors, however, had to be dug out of storage for this, as most theaters now used digital projectors. She had some leads on where to obtain film and what type of cameras had probably been used for the main reel and for those two spliced-in frames.

But it was showtime now; she had to switch gears. She pulled into her driveway and smiled at Major's welcoming bark. Emerging from her vehicle, she gave herself ten minutes to decompress and simply play with her dog.

Major was ecstatic. He did his circus-dog thing, dancing around on his hind legs for a length of time that had always amazed her, paws gently clawing the air. She threw tennis balls for him to chase, then had a rowdy session of tug-of-war, complete with growls from both of them. Finally, Major tired and dropped the thick rope, then made for his water dish and slurped noisily.

Jade settled on the bottom step of her tiny concrete porch and looked around. When this operation was over, she would plant flowers in pots. She'd been researching names and had a growing list: Mexican heather, salvia, marigolds. Maybe rosemary, too, since another project on the horizon was learning to cook with fresh herbs. The prime requirement for her was a plant that could handle Austin's intense summer heat without needing tons of water—first, because her schedule was too erratic, and second, because she wanted to be a good steward of natural resources.

Other criteria included having flowers, if possible—and not being easy to kill. She hadn't had a lot of luck with her first attempts at houseplants until she'd discovered plain old ivy.

Now there was an ideal greenery for a cop's schedule. It could handle abuse.

A swipe of Major's tongue over her hand yanked her out of daydreams. She glanced at her watch and leaped to her feet, pausing only long enough to scratch his ears and hug his furry head. "I'm sorry, boy. It's going to be another late night, but I'll get home as soon as I can. And in the morning, we'll go for a run."

Major spotted a squirrel and took off, obviously not too worried.

Jade watched him and vowed that one day he'd have lots of room to race around. Then she sighed, knowing how lucky she'd be to afford a tiny house with a miniscule yard.

But everyone had to start somewhere.

Tonight, however, she had to get her behind into gear. She unlocked the back door and headed for her closet.

Forty-five minutes later, cursing traffic, she pulled into the parking lot and emerged from her car in a run. She and Alex might have reached détente, but she wouldn't assume it would buy her any room to show up late.

She hit a low spot, and her ankle twisted in the lofty platform sandals. Muttering, she slowed down only slightly.

"Yo, Jade," Sean called out. "Your mama never taught you not to run in heels?"

She kept going, tossing a response over her shoulder. "These aren't heels." And she didn't discuss her mother.

He reached past her to open the door. "You're nearly as tall as me in them—I sure wouldn't call them flats."

"They don't make me throw my back out like those ice picks last night. They're flatter, just…elevated."

"You're telling me. Half the guys in the bar will be able to stand and still see up your skirt."

"It's not that short." She'd stopped inside the door, concentrating as she rotated her ankle, relieved to feel only a slight twinge.

"It's damn sure not long. 'Course, maybe they'll be too busy checking out the belly shirt—whoa there. You got a belly ring?"

"It's fake." She shuddered. "No way I'm letting anyone stick needles in me."

Sean's gaze climbed up her body. "You look good, Jade. Maybe too good."

"Not to catch a killer." She thought about Alex's kid sister and so many other innocent coeds, including two whose families were trapped in limbo. "I'd rather be in jeans, but…whatever it takes. DeDe Fairchild didn't deserve what happened to her."

"Yeah." Then he grinned as they walked through the door together. "Wear this outfit on our first date?"

"You bet," she shot back, watching his jaw drop. "I hear it's hot where you'll be the day I agree to go out with you."

Catcalls circled the room. "Busted, Sean," said one voice.

"Forget the technique lessons, Lover Boy," Bob jeered. "I can do better than that. Nail him again, Jade."

She took a brief bow, then proffered Sean a friendly smile.

Sean grinned back. "She wants me."

Hoots and laughter ensued.

Until Alex entered.

He cautioned himself that they were only letting off steam. No one on the team had to be reminded that they were here for a very serious purpose—every one of them would go to the wall to break this case open. Cops survived the pressures of their jobs in a variety of ways, not all of them healthy for their bodies. Humor was a sorely needed and innocuous escape valve.

And Jade had just proven, once again, that she could handle herself.

So why did he want to snap Sean's head off?

One look at her as she sauntered around the table was plenty. Her hot-pink shirt was tight and cropped just above her navel, displaying the lush curve of hip and breast and waist to advantage. The denim skirt hit her above mid-thigh, revealing most of the long shapely legs. Her hair tumbled down her back in a mass of waves, and at her navel winked a gold ring that matched the ones in her ears.

She looked good enough to eat.

He had no business noticing. She was a fellow cop, only doing the job they'd brought her over to accomplish.

So he cleared his throat and began the briefing.

Chapter Six

N ight Dreams was a new club located not on Sixth Street itself, but on a nearby, less attractive block where rents weren't quite so stratospheric. On the east side of it was an air-conditioning supply shop that had been in place since the fifties; adjoining it on the west was a vacant mechanic shop. The other beauty of the two missing girls, Tanya Marsalis, had vanished here. According to her friends, she had been almost frighteningly bright, with a taste for experimentation and walking on the edge.

Jade crossed her legs on the bar stool, alert for levels of interest as she sipped at her beer. She made periodic, obvious checks of her watch to further the impression that she was waiting for someone.

From his table, Alex kept vigil, scanning the room continuously for suspicious movement or undue interest in her.

Drawn, again and again, back to her himself.

A match flare against darkness, she was so alive, so vivid, so...

Exposed. And not just the too-tempting expanse of bare skin or the smooth swell of hip and breast, the endless legs. She probably worried over the curvaceous figure that didn't conform to current ideals of boyish lines, but she was everything a woman should be, as ripe and succulent as a June peach.

The artist in him wanted to paint her almost as much as the man wanted to touch.

She threw back her head and laughed, abundant auburn waves dancing across her back. He could see the effect on the current subject, having felt the lure of it himself, belly-tugging low.

Heads turned in her direction, and once again he surveyed the remaining team members' locations, knowing that they were all too far away to protect her completely.

He spotted Sean flirting with a table of girls, his back turned to Jade. Alex frowned until he registered Sean's eyes constantly roving the room, returning often to a mirror on the wall opposite, in which Jade's reflection was clear.

He pulled his gaze away and sought out Evan and Marco, listening with one ear to Jade's conversation, wishing the unit were on her rather than in the purse sitting beside her elbow on the bar.

A guy walked up beside her and tapped the wood for the bartender's attention, then leaned toward her. "Come here often?"

Jade resisted a smirk. *Oh, yeah. Original.* "This is my first time. You?" She fluttered her lashes and caught his perusal traveling from her legs to her chest. Instead of popping his chin upward as she'd like to do, she waited for his eyes to complete the journey.

"Wha—uh, yeah. I've been here before. Great sound system. Crowd's hopping most nights."

The bartender came for his order. The guy turned to her. "You want something?"

She lifted her glass. "No, thanks."

For a few minutes, she engaged in conversation while trying to solicit information about her friend Tanya, but nothing hit. Then his date, apparently tired of his delay, tapped his shoulder and retrieved him.

Jerk. Jade silently willed the woman to get a clue and ditch him. She uncrossed and recrossed her legs slowly. In seconds, another guy moved in.

He nodded toward the last man and shook his head. "Loser." He grinned. "I don't have a girlfriend with me."

"Where is she tonight?"

He seemed startled. "No, I don't—there's no—"

Jade couldn't help laughing. She engaged in byplay for a few minutes, then excused herself with murmurs about the bathroom, and changed her location. She was examining the crowd when someone brushed her right side. She turned just as a familiar face registered the shock that must be on her own.

Dan Fleming's eyes widened. "What are you doing here, Jade?"

"Hey, Dan—great to see you." She covered her reaction quickly.

Someone jostled him, tipping his balance onto the right leg, where she'd noticed he had a pronounced limp.

She steadied him. "Are you hurt?"

He stiffened. "I'm okay, just…surprised to see you." His eyes skimmed her attire. "Wow." Then he blushed. "Sorry. It's just—" He rolled his eyes. "Well, don't I sound articulate? So—you here with someone?"

She glanced around them. The noise level was such that eavesdropping wasn't likely. They could barely hear each other.

Before she could speak, she saw comprehension hit.

"Oh. You're—"

She smiled. Nodded.

"Oh, man. What, uh—you want me to just walk away

or—"

His discomfort was charming. She'd guess him to be close to her age, but trusting and openhearted in a way she hadn't been in years.

She placed a hand on his arm to stay his departure. "Not right this second. Nothing abrupt, okay? We'll just talk a minute as if we're old friends, then you tell me you're meeting someone and we'll say our goodbyes."

She raised her voice. "It's amazing to see you again. How's everything going?"

I'm sorry, he mouthed. "It's good. I'm…good." He leaned to speak in her ear. "How do you do this? I feel really awkward."

She spoke close to his ear. "Gets easier with practice." She leaned back, laughing, and delivered a playful slap to his shoulder. "You are so funny," she said loudly. "It's really great to run into you. You meeting someone?"

"Actually, I am. I'd better go, since I can't see the door from here. Listen, it was great to cross paths. We'll have to get together." He pulled a card from his pocket and scrawled a number on the back. "Here's my home phone. Give me a call, and we'll grab a drink after work sometime."

He rose, then leaned forward to kiss her cheek.

She went still. "You don't have to carry it that far."

"Who says I'm acting?" His grin was open and friendly. With a wave, he moved heavily toward the hostess stand.

Jade watched him go, then steeled herself to scout out her next mark.

Suddenly, Sean appeared before her, smiling for effect, but his eyes were solemn. He nodded toward the hall leading to the rest rooms. After a pause, she followed.

"What's up?"

"Alex's rounding up the troops. We've got another one."

She blew out a breath. "Where?"

"Industrial park. North this time."

"One of our girls, right?"

He nodded. "Tanya Marsalis. Same posing."

"Oh, man."

"Yeah. He wants us meeting in five minutes. You gonna leave first?"

"Okay." She turned to go, then reversed. "Wait—then the videotape's the same, too?"

"That's the word. Why?"

"Dan Fleming was just here." At his blank stare, she explained. "The DPS lab guy I consulted about the video images. I might be able to catch him. Maybe he'd see something at the scene we'd miss. Think Alex would like for him to come, too?"

"Don't know. He already gone?"

"He said he was meeting someone. I think he's still around."

"Let me check." He pulled out his cell phone and hit speed dial.

Jade slid away from him and studied a poster on the wall to avoid appearing to be with him.

After a brief conversation, Sean disconnected. "He said bring him if you can find him, but don't take long. I'll come behind you."

Jade nodded and began to search. She located Dan near the hostess stand and tapped him on the shoulder. "Dan?"

"Hey. What's up?"

"Your date not here yet?"

"She's not really a date. More of a friend."

"Listen, you don't have to do this, since she'll be expecting you, but—" Jade glanced around them, then drew him back into a corner and leaned close to his ear. "We just got a call. There's another girl, found the same way as the first one."

He reared back. "Dead? Another one's—"

"Hush." She frowned hard at him. "Keep it down."

He blanched. "Sorry." Hands on hips, he drew in a deep breath. "It's just that—Well, my work is all in the lab, see, and—" His forehead wrinkled. "Wait—you mean—What are you asking, Jade?"

"You're under no obligation, but I was thinking that maybe, with your background, you'd notice something the rest of us might not." She shook her head. "It won't be pretty, Dan. There's no shame if you're not up to it."

Indecision danced over his features for a minute, then his jaw firmed. "No, that would be wrong. I saw the other girl in those two shots I recovered. She looked so alive and eager—she didn't deserve what happened to her. If another one is—" His gaze flew to hers. "I've never been to a crime scene."

"I can't force you to go to this one. I wouldn't if I could."

"No need. I'll do what's right." He grabbed the cell phone off his belt and flipped it open, then hit a number on his speed dial. After a few seconds, he spoke. "Hi, it's me. Listen, something's come up with work. I've got to go. Where are you?" As he listened, his mouth curved. "For once, it's good that you're never on time. How about later in the week?"

Jade swiveled away to let him finish his conversation in private. When Sean crossed her vision, eyebrows lifted, she nodded. He signaled that he'd wait for her outside.

"Okay." Dan slid his phone back in the holder. "I'm ready."

"This way," she said, then paused with one hand on his arm. "But if you change your mind, no judging on our parts. No one does that great with their first dead body. You just handle it as best you can."

He was a little pale, but he nodded and followed her outside.

Alex tuned out the crime scene techs setting up lights on the perimeter. They would delay, he knew, as long as he insisted, but they'd been dragged from their beds and would be eager to return.

The rest of the bystanders, the uniforms who'd responded to the anonymous tip from a burner phone, the sector supervisor and homicide detectives, along with his own team, would hold—not patiently, perhaps, and not without resentment—until he gave the command.

And he'd give it, but first he would take another minute or two to absorb impressions, sort out any differences. He'd seen far more violent deaths than most anyone who stood at his back, certainly more victims of serial killings.

Which now, indisputably, they had. He'd expected from the first victim that there would be more, but he'd hoped to be wrong.

He cataloged details to take out later, adjusting for the discrepancy in time of day they were viewing the scene. Death always appeared more natural, somehow, in the half world of darkness, though it also had greater impact on the psyche.

No matter how hardened he'd become, he hoped he'd never get easy with the sights and smells of man's brutality. The day he did, he would know that the bad guys had won.

"Okay." He stepped back and nodded to the techs. "It's all yours."

They swung into action with careful steps, photographing the area first before walking over any possible evidence.

Alex sought out his team and found them ranged around

the perimeter in spots chosen for best viewing from a variety of perspectives they'd compare later. Satisfaction surged through him. They were a good crew.

Just then, he noted a disturbance off to one side and frowned at the fair-haired stranger who stood between Jade and Sean, his face pale, sweat dotting his brow. Arms crossed over his stomach, he sucked in a deep breath while Jade placed a hand on his arm and spoke to him, worry on her features. She tugged as if to urge him away, but he shook her off and focused on the victim.

Alex didn't think the guy, who must be the DPS video expert, had ever seen a dead body in person before. Probably lots of them in photos, but that wasn't the same thing. Photos conferred the ability to retain objectivity that real life didn't allow.

But he held, to his credit. Not easily, yet he did better than some rookies. And he hadn't blown Jade's cover in the bar.

Alex decided not to focus on the flirting this kid had done. Every man who'd crossed her path had reacted the same way. It was just that she'd responded warmly in this one instance. He shook off the irritation and cut the fellow some slack, giving him a breather by interposing his body between the guy and the scene.

"Hey, Alex," Sean greeted.

"Sean, Jade." He purposely avoided looking at Jade, this close to her. Instead, he held out a hand. "I'm Alex Sandoval, FBI."

The blond cleared his throat and stuck out his own. "Dan Fleming from DPS."

Alex refrained from commenting on Fleming's obvious discomfort, understanding that giving him a chance to switch his reaction to analysis instead of emotion would be the best break he could hand the guy, short of sending him home. "Talk to me about your impressions."

Gratitude flared. "I haven't seen the previous crime scene photos, but—"

Alex held up his hand. "That can be remedied." He turned. "Bob, can you grab my laptop?"

"Sure thing." Bob left for the car he and Alex had shared on the way over.

Alex focused on Fleming again. "Want to wait to see them before you say anything?"

"I can do that, but tell me this first. The basic pose is the same?"

"Yes."

"I thought so."

Alex frowned. "Why's that?"

"I've seen this pose before."

"Where?"

Fleming held up a hand. "Not in my job. In a film."

"Which one?"

"Probably none you've ever seen. I went to film school for two and a half years, and students pay little attention to the blockbusters—at least, as far as they'll admit." He grinned. "They're *auteurs*, you dig? Artists whose medium is film, not hacks who've sold out to the system." He glanced up and no doubt saw the impatience Alex was feeling. "Sorry. Anyway, I'm not sure where it was, but I've run across this pose before."

"Who made it?"

"Good question. I think it was at a student film festival, but I've been out of school for a while. If I noted the director's name, I've forgotten it."

"That's not good enough," Alex said. "I need to know who it was, who was part of the production, where they are now—" He broke off. "Tell me it wasn't a snuff film." If it was one of the far-out fringe for sexual sadists who would pay big money for movies with actual deaths on them, the situation was beyond serious.

"No. No way. Festival organizers would have weeded it out if that had been the case."

"Unless they weren't told. The concept of artistic freedom gets pushed pretty far by some elements."

Fleming uttered a sound of protest, but Alex ignored it when he spotted Bob approaching with his laptop. Alex opened the case and booted it up, tapping his fingers as he waited, then used the trackpad to pull up the image he wanted. "Here." He turned the computer toward Fleming, watching his eyes as he studied it.

Fleming's eyes were steady now as he engaged in a more normal activity for him: analyzing from a picture. "Same basic pose," he muttered, then lifted his head. "How soon can you shoot me copies?"

"I'll call it in right now."

"I'll head to my office and wait to get them. I need my big displays to get the best perspective."

"In the meantime, be thinking about dates and places where you saw that movie."

"I will." Fleming turned, then halted. "I forgot. I don't have my car."

"I'll drive him," Jade offered.

"That'd be great—" Fleming began.

"No—" Alex interrupted. "You stay here, Jade. We'll get a uniform to do it."

She cast Fleming an expression of apology.

"I'll phone you tomorrow, Jade," Fleming said.

She smiled. "I'd like that."

"Contact me first with your report," Alex snapped.

And ground his teeth.

Chapter Seven

After only four hours' sleep, Jade was punchy. Never had she needed Trey's magic more. She made her way up the steps of the old house he and co-owner Steve had converted, reacting like one of Pavlov's dogs as the coffee smell hit her.

Behind the counter, Trey grinned. "You look terrible."

"Don't waste time talking to me." But she smiled back, holding out her arm. "Just get out the IV and pump it straight in."

He laughed and instantly produced the giant-size cup she'd been dreaming of since the alarm went off.

"You magician, you," she sighed. "How did you know?"

One shoulder lifted. "Got this sixth sense. Tells me when my favorite cop is in dire straits and on her way."

She didn't respond for a second, too busy sucking down caffeine, scorched tongue notwithstanding. Pain couldn't make a dent this morning. Exhaustion had all the bases covered.

"Leave your wife, Trey. She can't possibly need you as much as I do."

He chuckled. His devotion to his family was common knowledge. He waved a pound of her favorite blend in her face. "You were out, right? Did I hit it?"

"Smart aleck." She held out a hand. "I have no idea why I argue."

"Me, either. Makes me feel like I'm at home, though. Anything else?"

She realized the line behind her was growing rapidly. "Nope. I'll live now, thanks to you."

"You could stand to eat something with that, Jade. Breakfast is the most important meal, after all."

"Thanks, Mom." She didn't want anything for herself but bought a selection of the decadent pastries. Bob and Sean, for sure, would be grateful.

When she walked into VICTAF headquarters, she wasn't surprised to find the place already humming with activity. After they discovered what she was carrying, she received two proposals of marriage and three of a less respectable nature. Before the horde swooped in, she selected two of the best and put them on a paper towel.

"No fair," Sean complained. "I'm bigger than you. I need more calories."

"Tough it out, Romeo. Good for you to hear a woman say no." To a chorus of hoots, she walked down the hall, grinning.

At the door to Alex's office, she paused and battled nerves.

He'd been cold and distant last night, but it hadn't been a time for anything but business. Still, yesterday they'd shared something approaching friendship.

She stepped into the opening. He was on the phone and busy taking notes.

About to leave, she caught a glimpse of the pad. It wasn't notes.

Alex was doodling.

Just then, he glanced her way. She backed up, signaling

Never mind.

He shook his head and waved her inside, gestured her to take a seat.

As he wrapped up the call, she sneaked a peek at him. *Mamma mia,* he was gorgeous, not in a poster boy sense like Sean but...compelling. Strong bones, the carved lines and angles of maturity.

And dangerous. Something dark and edgy hovered like an aura.

She couldn't take her eyes off him.

But you'd better, Jade. He's all cop, and he won't thank you for it.

So she dragged her gaze from his face and cocked her head to see what he was doodling—then realized it was much more than absent scribbles.

A woman's face, beautifully drawn. Bold, clean lines shouting confidence. Experience. No wasted motion.

Jade's eyes nearly popped out as she puzzled over this new information. He was an artist, a very talented one. Easy to tell that, even upside down. She wished fervently that she could examine the drawing closer.

Then inspiration struck. She rose and rounded the desk to place the pastries beside him—

And bobbled them when realization hit her.

The face was her own.

Just then, he hung up.

She scrambled to retreat, banging her hip hard into the desk corner. And gasped at the impact.

"You all right?" he asked.

"Yeah, sure." She backed up. "I'm fine. Fine. I, uh—this isn't a fair trade for lunch, but I thought you might like—" *Stop babbling, Jade.*

"Thanks." He reached for a pastry, then froze as his own gaze landed on the drawing.

In that moment, conflicting impulses seized her. She had the urge to disappear to escape the tension that suddenly filled the room.

She also wanted to know why he was drawing her.

And how he could make her look so...amazing.

Her gaze met his, then darted away.

His hand slowly closed, crumpling the drawing. Without thinking, she grabbed for it, her hand covering his. Sending jitters when they touched.

His eyes locked on hers. She couldn't move.

And for a second, all the air in the room seemed to vanish.

Bob's voice sounded outside. "Alex's office is on the right."

Jade longed to force him to relinquish the drawing, but he rose, crushing it in his fist. She opened her mouth to speak, though she hadn't the slightest clue what she would say—

Dan Fleming knocked on the door frame. "Hey, great. You're both here. Listen, I'm headed home to sleep now, but I've got something you might want to see."

And just like that, Alex became Agent Sandoval. Jade's reactions were slower, and she mourned the loss of an opportunity that would never come again.

"Let's take a look." Alex chunked the paper at the trash can, and Jade followed its arc.

Then she blinked and gathered her wits.

"Hey, Jade." Dan grinned, perusing her slacks and tailored shirt. "I liked the other outfit better."

If the atmosphere had been chilly before, it plummeted to subarctic now. "Having been up all night, you surely have better things to do than talk wardrobes." Alex's tone was sharp. "What have you got for me?"

Dan cast her a startled glance. She shrugged back.

He proffered one photo. "The second reel was full of garbage, an oddly-spliced montage with no apparent theme, but I retrieved one image. It might be a leap, but part of the background makes me wonder if this might be our first crime scene."

Alex was already studying the picture. Jade craned her neck, trying to see past his broad shoulders. As she leaned, she brushed his arm, and he jolted.

"Sorry."

"Go ahead." The second she touched the photo, he stepped to the side and put distance between them.

She caught Dan's eyes darting from her to Alex and back before she shoved away her embarrassment and focused on the print. "It could be," she mused. "But it's so dark."

Dan shifted uncomfortably. "Getting that much wasn't easy. I had to do a lot of enhancement to make it clearer."

She lifted her gaze to his and smiled. "I didn't mean to sound ungrateful."

He returned the print. "I never saw the first place, but the wall caught my attention. I pulled the pictures you sent over and enhanced them for clarity, too, and there's a strong similarity between the warehouse in which the first victim was found and the wall in that photo."

"I want to send all the recovered footage to the FBI labs. They've got the latest equipment. They might be able to capture more off the reels."

"But I—" Dan halted.

"We don't have the luxury of ego, Fleming. You've done good work, and we appreciate it, but we need as much as we can obtain."

"I can get you more."

"Then why haven't you?"

"Because more takes time. And different equipment the

lab doesn't have." Dan straightened, his voice filled with quiet pride. "But I have access to other stuff."

Alex's eyes narrowed. "You also have a workload."

"I saw that girl." Dan's voice wobbled, then firmed. "There's another one still missing, and a whole lot more potential victims walking around this town."

Jade peered at Alex, thinking about his kid sister. He kept his face carefully impassive, but she suspected he was right there with her.

Dan's chin lifted. "If I can do something to help stop this guy, that has to be priority. If I have to take vacation days to concentrate on this case, I will."

Alex shook his head. "I doubt it will be necessary. I'll speak to your supervisor." Then he relented a bit. "Head home for now and grab some sleep. You'll miss important details if you're too exhausted."

"I can go as long as anyone else."

Dan's pride was dinged. Jade wondered about the limp and how often he'd been treated as weak because of it.

Alex's tone held nothing of pity. "The rest of the team managed at least a few hours. You take the morning and catch up."

Dan's face lit when Alex's words included him as part of them. "Yeah, okay. I guess I could use a couple of winks."

"Give me a call when you're up and around. I'll want you to confer with the FBI lab, coordinate resources. If necessary, I'll send you to D.C."

Dan's eyes widened then. "Oh, wow. Cool." She could almost see him rubbing his hands with glee.

"But not until you sleep."

"Yeah, okay. I'm gone." At the doorway, he paused. "Uh, Jade? You got a minute?"

Standing beside Alex, she froze. "Maybe later." She slid

Alex a sideways glance.

"We're through here." His face revealed nothing, but disapproval shouted from his stance.

Inwardly wincing, she followed Dan out in the hall.

"Listen, um…are you involved with anyone?"

"Involved?"

"Yeah, you know, dates. Dinner."

"Oh." As what he was asking sank in, she was slow to respond.

Color rose on his throat. "Never mind. It was a stupid idea." He turned to leave.

He might have experience with rejection. "Wait." She caught him in two steps. "I'm sorry. It's—I'm just slow on the uptake." She smiled to remove the sting.

His gaze dipped to his leg, then rose, filled with challenge. "Some women—"

She didn't let him finish. "I'm not most women." Then decided to hit dead on. "I couldn't care less about your leg, unless you can't forget it."

His shoulders relaxed slightly. His eyes lit with humor. "I don't let it get in my way, not anymore." He paused. "In any sense."

Now it was her turn to blush. "I, uh—"

Dan chuckled, then let her off the hook. "Dinner would be a good start."

Her gaze shifted to Alex's office. "My nights are a little busy right now."

"I'll accept a rain check."

Just then, Alex emerged from his office. "Butler, if you can spare a minute from your social life, I need your report on last night."

"Yes, sir." Furious discomfort rushed up her throat, over her face.

"Ouch," Dan said quietly. "Sorry about that."

"Forget it. He'd love nothing better than to get me busted back to Sex Crimes." She bared her teeth. "But he's doomed to disappointment."

"My bet's on you."

She swerved her focus. "It shouldn't be. He has seniority, and he's the almighty FBI. I'm only on loan."

"You're not paying attention, Jade."

"What does that mean?" Her brow wrinkled.

"Only that it's not your work that's bugging him." He turned away. "But before you wind up in hot water again, I'd better go."

"Wait—"

Dan halted.

She caught up to him. "A rain check works for me."

"Deal." He was smiling as he left.

Still puzzling over his allusion, she headed back to face the music.

"Close the door, Detective."

She frowned but complied. "Sir, I don't believe I've done anything wrong, but—"

"Have I accused you of any wrongdoing?" His fierce golden eyes blazed, but his voice was neutral.

"You said—" She paused. It was more his tone that made her feel vaguely guilty. "No, sir. Not in so many words, but I thought—" Too much conflicting input rocketed around in her head. "May I speak frankly, sir?"

"How many times do I have to tell you that we don't stand on protocol around here? I thought we were past the *sirs*." He sighed. "Speak your mind."

"I don't know what you want from me." Confusion mushroomed into anger. "You warn me, then you act friendly. You bust my chops, then you give me credit. And you—" She cast her glance at the empty pad on his desk. "Never mind."

He uttered a low, rueful sound. "I wish you weren't here."

At her gasp, he held up a hand. "You wanted honesty—you got it. My life would be a whole lot simpler if you were back at APD, but the requirements of this case are paramount, and—" His gaze pinned hers. "You're good at what you do. Not just the undercover." He frowned. "You have the brains, and you think outside the box. Half of catching guys like this is methodical attention to detail. The other half is intuition and the ability to crawl inside their minds."

She was rooted to the floor as amazement flooded in. This kind of praise meant everything to her. "Thank you, sir—Alex," she corrected.

"Don't thank me yet." His expression was grim. "We have a long way to go on this case, and your situation grows steadily more dangerous. You've got to be on your toes every second."

"I know my job," she sniffed.

"I never assumed you were given that shield just for being a pretty face, Detective." His phone rang. "I'd better take this."

"Sure thing." She moved to the door.

"Jade—"

She looked back and caught an odd expression on his face. "Yes?"

"Nothing." He shook his head. "You have another undercover stint tonight. Get some rest this afternoon."

"I'm not tired."

Her eyes were clear and bright, her body all but vibrating. If she were any more eager, he'd need an anchor to hold her to earth.

"You will be by midnight. I'm sending everybody home for some down time this afternoon, so don't feel insulted." He turned to grab another file.

"How about you?"

He glanced over his shoulder, lifting an eyebrow. "What about me?"

"Will you have time off, too?"

"Detective, I don't believe that's any concern of yours."

"Your head needs to be clear just as much as ours do. Maybe more."

Alex wasn't accustomed to being cared for. "I've been at this awhile. I know what my body—and brain—require. At any rate, I have a date with the coroner."

"I understand my own requirements, as well. Let me go with you."

He cocked his head. "You ever attended an autopsy?"

"Once."

"During training?"

She nodded.

"How'd you do?"

Her chin jutted. "I held."

He smiled. "I'll bet you did." He turned away again. "What time?"

"What?" He pulled his attention back to her.

"What time shall I be ready?"

He exhaled. "You always this much of an eager beaver?"

"Top of my class, teacher's pet—the whole bit."

He shook his head. "Be ready at twelve. We'll grab a bite first."

"Okay." She sprinted up from her chair.

"Oh, Jade?"

She paused at the door. "Yes?"

"You're right. The pastries don't count. It's still your treat."

Pleasure blossomed in her expression. "But you get paid

more."

He shrugged, surprised to be enjoying himself this much. "That's the way the cookie crumbles."

With a cheery wave, she departed.

Chapter Eight

S he directed him to Steve and Trey's place, Twisted
Chimney, where they served sandwiches and soups a
thousand times better than the courthouse swill.

It wasn't that far off their path, she told herself.

Okay, so she was showing off. "I could drive, you know."

Alex dipped his head in acknowledgment. "Yeah, but
mine's got legroom."

He was right about that. The big, shiny black SUV beat
the daylights out of her economy model in any number of
ways. "One of your confiscated vehicles?"

"Nope." He twisted, looking behind him as he slid it into
a parking place with one expert move.

"Impressive."

He straightened the wheels and grinned. "All in the
wrists."

She laughed, stemming the flutter that smile provoked
with such ease. "I meant the car—okay, I lied. Parallel parking
was my undoing on the driving test. But the car's slick, too."

He shrugged. "Meets my needs. I like to hit the back
trails, and at home, the terrain can be rough."

They slipped between vehicles. It wasn't the lunch rush,
thank goodness, but the Chimney never really got quiet. "You
said you grew up in West Texas?"

"Little village called La Paloma, then later in Alpine." He held the door for her.

The remote locale fit the hard angles of him. She handed him a menu as they stood in line before the counter. "I'm still surprised."

"About what?"

"You mentioned a brother who's older, but you act like an eldest child."

"Bossy, you mean?" He nodded. "They'd all agree. What do you like here?" he asked, scanning the menu.

"The Santa Fe. But I didn't mean bossy. You're more…protective."

His eyebrows rose. "A nice way to put it. Liam wasn't quite so diplomatic during his recent excitement."

She frowned and searched her memory. Then had it. "Oh yeah. He got stabbed, someplace back east. He's all right now, isn't he?"

"Are you asking as a fan?"

She heard it again, the guardian's tone. "I was asking because he's your brother and you obviously love him." She shrugged. "You got a problem with talking about him, no skin off my nose."

"Ouch. Your turn." He gestured for her to order.

She hadn't even noticed that they'd moved to the front of the line.

"Hey, girl. How'd the pastries go down at the cop shop?"

"Ask him, Steve. He had two."

Alex smiled. "I plan to remember where this place is. It could be on my way without any sweat."

"Good, good." Smiling as always, Steve stood at the ready. "What can I get two of APD's finest?"

Jade opened her mouth to point out that Alex was FBI until he shook his head. They ordered and paid, then found a table to wait for their food.

"Sorry about being defensive earlier," Alex said. "I spent too many hours fighting off half the media in the known world, along with multitudes of fans holding vigils, waiting for Liam's PR team to arrive and take over." He paused. "Liam pays a price for his celebrity. We try to make sure that we aren't contributing to it."

She looked at him. "It must be so weird—I mean, he's your kid brother, right? So you probably changed his diapers and saw him pick his nose, but women all over the world are sighing over this guy. You have to take him down to size often?"

He laughed then, free and easy. "There are plenty of us to go around."

"You're a close family, even though you don't all have the same father."

"Absolutely. Dad may not be my biological father, but no kid ever had a better one. He's this big guy, all hail-fellow-well-met. Liam's a lot like him, come to think of it. Dad took a widow and two boys who were a handful, and he not only welcomed us but never let us feel that we were less important to him than the kids he and Mom had together. He's a hell of a guy."

"So what about your mom?" Try as she might, Jade had never solved the mystery of mothers. Hers had been strong enough to bring her into the world, but too weak to stand alone after that. "I guess she was grateful that he was there to rescue her."

He burst into full-throated laughter, and it was a revelation. "Oh, man, I wish the rest of the family could hear that—sorry." He stifled his chuckles. "My mother is the smallest one in the family, barely five-two, but if you want to know who everyone's terrified of, it's her."

Jade frowned. "How do you mean that?"

His eyes warmed to caramel. "I can't explain it. She's a lady, through and through. She would never harm anyone—well, unless they threatened her family. She doesn't need to." He shook his head. "She just—somehow, no matter what you thought you were set on, you'd give up everything, do anything, to please her. And you'd rather take a bullet than disappoint her." There was nothing of fear and everything of admiration in his tone. "She's the strongest, most loving woman I've ever met, and every one of us would walk through fire for her."

Wow. A paragon. Jade thanked the server who brought their food and dug in, but her thoughts traveled to her grandmother, who could be described with many of those words. Ladylike. Strong.

But loving…no.

"What about you? You went to live with relatives, didn't you, after—" He fell silent, and the atmosphere suddenly turned uncomfortable.

"My grandparents on my mother's side. I never knew who my dad was. If my mother did, she wouldn't say."

"That's tough. My father's mother was—and is—a very important figure in our lives. Were they good to you?"

Jade shrugged. "I made it." She saw it then, that haunted expression he'd worn before. "Don't."

"Don't what?"

"It was fine. I managed."

The atmosphere, so recently free and easy, became stiff. His face closed down.

She mourned it. "Listen, they fed me and clothed me. I got through school, made a life for myself."

"You felt alone. Why?"

She didn't talk about this stuff. With anyone. If she'd seen pity in his eyes, she wouldn't have said one more word. "They didn't want my mother to keep me. They cut off all contact when she did."

"She must have been quite a woman."

Jade had puzzled over that often. "It required courage to defy them. I still don't know where she found it. Mostly I remember her being scared to death of the world." She tore her bread to pieces. "She loved me, I guess, but she always needed a man around. Any man."

"You don't." He didn't make it a question.

She lifted her gaze to his. "No. And I won't." She sipped her iced tea, then scooted her chair back. "I guess we'd better go."

He studied her; she refused to look. She didn't want to see if pity had crept in after all.

Finally, he crumpled his napkin and rose. "You don't have to do this."

"Yes," she said. "I do."

"All right." He followed her to the door and opened it before she could. His hand rested, for one second, lightly at the small of her back. "After you."

Jittering from his touch more than from their destination, she chanced a peek then, but he appeared unmoved.

That was just fine with her. Better, in fact. Because, for a few minutes, she'd gotten unsettled hearing a man talk about his family, a close and painful glimpse inside the world of her dreams.

And they'd never seemed farther away.

When they left the medical examiner's office, Jade was

distinctly pale.

But she'd held, just as she'd promised. The experience had been a painful reminder of the stakes for all of them—young girls whose lives had been snuffed out before they'd barely begun. Potential wasted, families sundered.

And danger in store, for other girls as yet unknown.

Danger for Jade.

Her beautiful face was set and strained. He wanted to go back to those few moments when they'd laughed and talked, when there'd been rapport between them. She should spend all her days that way, young and carefree. Instead, she was part of a manhunt, delectable bait being dangled for a madman. She should be starting a storybook life with some guy who would worship the ground she walked on and be eager to put babies in her belly, spend happy years with their children as a soccer mom in a minivan—

The chuckle burst from him without warning.

Her head whipped around. "What can you possibly find humorous?" The green eyes snapped, and he realized that she wasn't frightened.

She was furious.

She'd be more so if he explained. "Nothing. Sorry. It wasn't related."

"What happened to her—it's so wrong." Her voice was nearly a growl. "I'm ready for tonight. I'm going to find him."

He stopped in the middle of the sidewalk and jerked her around to face him. "You won't take chances. You're part of a team, and this isn't on you to catch him. If you can't remember that, you know what I'll do."

"What about your sister? Think she can't be the next one? How can you just stand there so calmly?"

Thoughts of Jilly, with her sassy smile that wouldn't quit, her irrepressible joy in living, sent icy dark fingers into his gut.

But that didn't change things. Passions made you stupid, tripped you up. "If you can't be objective, you're an obstacle, not an asset, Detective."

She yanked her arm from his and stabbed a finger back toward the building. "That girl should be at Barton Springs today or shopping with her friends or hanging out in the library, flirting with boys." Her voice vibrated with outrage.

Then, right before his eyes, she crammed a lid on her emotions. Closed her eyes and sucked in one deep breath after another, hands clamped on her hips, knuckles white. "You're right," she said finally. "I know you're right. It's just that—"

Then her eyes opened, and he saw moisture in them, restrained with all the formidable power of her will.

Jade Butler would never shed tears over herself or the bad cards life had handed her. But these foolish girls who'd had so much more than anyone had ever given Jade…she would let herself feel for them.

In that moment, he was torn by two impulses: one, to open his arms to her as he would to Jilly, to comfort. It would embarrass her every bit as much as it would help.

His second temptation, however, kept him standing apart from her.

Because he found himself admiring her more every day.

And wanting her.

She exhaled sharply. "I apologize. If you could drive me back to my car, I'll go get ready."

He could see that she had herself in hand now. The necessity of a response from him was over without him having to figure out who would make it, the man or the cop. Her supervisor or the failed negotiator who'd handed her one of those bad cards.

He should be glad.

But he wasn't.

"You'll take two hours at home."

"I have work to do."

"That's an order, Detective."

She whirled and planted herself squarely in front of him. "You're not my guardian, and I haven't needed a mother in years. As a matter of fact, I don't need a ride, either. It's only six blocks to my car, and I could use the fresh air." She stepped around him, a full head of steam already building.

He grabbed her arm. "Detective—"

She shook him off.

He didn't grab her again. He didn't trust the temper he so seldom lost anymore. "Jade. Stop." He paused. "Please."

Finally, she complied, but she didn't turn.

"It gets to me, too, you know."

She said nothing, but he could tell she was listening by the set of her shoulders.

"You're too much like her," he said.

She turned. "Who?"

He grimaced. "Jilly. My sister. She's got reddish blond hair. And a hot head."

At last, her lips curved slightly. "That's a myth. Redheads are not hot-tempered. It's an old wives' tale."

"Couldn't prove it by me." He gestured toward his vehicle. "Let me give you a lift. You'll be on your feet plenty tonight." When she hesitated, he offered an olive branch. "Jilly never wanted to take naps, either."

She started walking toward him. "Just so you know, I happen to adore naps." She cast him a sideways glance. "Only not on command."

"Jilly is lousy with authority, too." He cranked up the engine.

She was only gone an hour, and most of that was travel and the time she spent playing with her dog. She paid a neighbor kid to exercise him when she was working, but he was her dog, after all, and he deserved as much of her attention as she could spare, even in the midst of a heavy case.

Alex would be ticked off, no doubt, but she wasn't being stubborn about sleep. She didn't require as much as some people, and anyway, she was too wound up for it now. She walked toward his office, thinking to get the dustup over with, when she heard the sounds of a heated exchange.

"One more night, and that's it, Doc. The undercover's not working. We should go at it from another angle."

"It's your call. What do you suggest?"

Alex's tone held frustration. "I wish I knew."

"Jade's doing a good job, isn't she?"

Jade held her breath for his answer.

"Yeah, but it's inefficient. We need more people in more locations. He might never return to these two bars."

"Or he might just be biding his time."

"Where's the third girl? What's he waiting for?"

"Maybe that one's not connected."

"I hope like hell she's not."

"But you don't think so."

"It breaks pattern, if Jade's theory is right."

"Perhaps it's not."

"None of the others fit the facts we have so far. The missing bouncer, Rick Howard, still hasn't turned up. If nothing happens tonight, we'll lay off a day or switch women."

Jade jolted into motion, but stopped herself before she

came into sight. *Think, Jade. What's your argument?* Somehow, she sensed that if she confronted him now, she'd be replaced immediately. Unless Doc stood up for her.

"You plan to send her back to APD, if that's the case?"

She was ready to charge again, when she heard Alex speak.

"I haven't decided. She's got a good head on her. We'll have to see how things play out." Then he switched gears. "What's happening on the warehouse searches?"

"APD is sparing uniforms whenever they can, but they don't have overtime budget for more."

"DeDe Fairchild was enrolled in a film class. Ben got that from one of her friends. I have him checking out the faculty."

Their voices drew nearer to the door. Jade roused herself to duck into the break room, her thoughts racing.

Tonight she had to make something happen. She was not letting them bring in another female officer to take her place. She hadn't been slacking, but she'd have to shake the tree harder and see if something—or someone—would drop out.

Alex was in Austin mode tonight, jeans and boots and a T-shirt, nursing a beer as he stood in a corner and observed the action.

And only with effort kept a scowl off his face.

Jade was pressing her luck. Not only her outfit, the skin-hugging jeans riding low on her hips, the tight tank top displaying her generous cleavage—she didn't need the showstopper legs uncovered to attract attention. She'd been a flower surrounded by hungry bees since the moment she walked in; he didn't have to hear the conversations coming through the unit concealed in her tiny crossbody purse to know that she'd received one come-on after another.

She was on the hunt tonight, and the males were circling her.

And that was before she'd started dancing.

No sedate sitting on a bar stool tonight—oh, no. Her hair was long and loose and shifting over her back, beckoning like flame, brushing the hands of the current target as they clasped her hips and pulled her close against him—

Alex barely stifled a growl. Only his awareness that the sound would be broadcast to every other officer in the room kept a lid on his ire.

And the person who needed to realize she'd pushed him about as far as she could was the only one who couldn't hear him. She was the only one without an earpiece.

"Whoa, buddy—slow down." Her laughter was husky, teasing as she placed her hands on the guy's hips and moved him enough to get space between their bodies. "Oof—hey!"

Alex craned to get a visual, just in time to see the guy grasp her hair and wind it around his wrist.

She kept her cool. "Let's take it off the dance floor, okay?"

Alex watched her shift her stance, but the guy's grip on her hair impeded her.

"I don't wanna leave." The man was drunk and slurring. Not likely their target, but still a potential problem if he forced Jade to best him, as Alex had no doubt she could.

"Hold, everyone," he said into his unit. "Give her a chance." But he put his beer down and started toward her. He could step in as a concerned bystander, if necessary, without blowing her cover.

"Back off, bud." Jade used a pressure point to force him to let go of her hair.

"Ow, bitch—" The guy withdrew for a second, looking as if he'd reconsidered his interest.

"What is that, a knife?" Jade's voice rose as if nervous, but Alex caught her shifting her weight to prepare for a defensive posture. "Hey, I didn't mean anything."

She was good, making sure all of them were alerted. She wouldn't let her cover slip, not yet.

"I'm on it. Everyone stay back," he ordered, rocking to his toes, ready to rush to the rescue.

Then all hell broke loose. The guy grabbed Jade's tank top between her breasts and yanked her close, brandishing the blade.

Someone screamed. People scrambled, blocking Alex's view.

"Evan, get a uniform in here to handle the arrest and pre-serve cover." Alex charged through the milling crowd, shoving bodies to the side until he could see Jade grappling with her attacker. One foot was readied to smash his instep, when a panicked dancer knocked her to the side, right into her assailant.

Three feet away now, Alex leaped, grabbing the guy's wrist and preventing another arc of the deadly knife. "Drop it, you bastard!"

Jade jerked out of the man's grasp.

Alex didn't let go but scanned her for signs of injury.

Her hands were clenched, her body poised to attack. She wasn't scared; she was spitting mad.

She glared at Alex and opened her mouth.

He shook his head in warning.

Reluctantly, she subsided, but her body language screamed how badly she wanted to wade into someone.

Alex held the struggling drunk and wondered if it was him or his captive she'd most like to battle.

Then the patrol officer arrived. "Break it up."

Alex held on longer than he should have.

"I've got him, sir. Step away. I'll sort this out."

Alex indicated Jade. "I saw this young lady having trouble, so I lent a hand to help her out."

"Don't leave," the patrolman commanded. "My partner will want to talk to both of you. Are you okay, miss?"

"I'm fine." But her voice wasn't steady.

Alex scrutinized her, and the man in him battled with the cop. One skinny strap of her tank top was broken, and the thin cotton was slipping down the curve of one breast.

"Paramedics should be on their way," the officer said as he cuffed the suspect. He spoke into the microphone clipped to his shoulder.

"I don't need them," Jade snapped.

"I'll stay with her, officer," Alex offered.

"All right. My partner will be here in a minute." He left with the cursing drunk.

Alex faced Jade. "Tell me the truth. Are you hurt?"

"I said I'm okay." She wouldn't look at him, each syllable clipped to a fine edge.

"I want you examined."

"No."

"It's not your decision."

Off to the side, paramedics waded through the people bunched at the door, and Alex motioned for them.

He turned back in time to spot Jade slipping into the crowd. "Damn it—" He plunged after her. "Evan, pull the patrol units aside. Tell them to talk to me tomorrow. Bob, gather everyone up for a briefing, then send them home."

"Jade okay?" Sean asked.

"She's not hurt," he snapped. "I'll see you all in the morning." Then he cut off his unit. What would likely ensue when he caught her was not a discussion for the rest of the team.

She was halfway down the alley after exiting through the back of the club when he grabbed her.

She swung around, ready for battle.

It suited him down to the ground, but he would not engage in a free-for-all here.

"Throw the switch on your unit." He'd already done the same on his own. He forced himself to step back. "And cool off."

"Cool—?" A gasp of disbelief. Her eyes narrowed, but she complied with the transmitter. "You ruined my op."

"It's not ruined. And it's not your op."

"I was handling him."

"He had you trapped. He pulled a blade on you." The memory of those fingers knotted in the fabric between her breasts, the knife menacing, wouldn't leave him soon.

"I can defend myself."

"With room to maneuver, probably, but the congestion hampered you. I couldn't risk it."

"You don't have to protect me. I'm not fifteen anymore, Alex."

"I know that." He did—it wasn't a girl he was remembering. "I didn't break your cover. Or mine."

"We could still be in there working if you hadn't waded in like some avenging angel."

That tore it. "Bullshit. You're shaking."

"It's just adrenaline." She raked unsteady fingers through her hair.

"You took chances tonight, Jade. You're trying too hard to draw attention, parading yourself around—" *The bastard pulled a knife on her.* Ruthlessly, he throttled the savagery bubbling just beneath the surface. "I told you I don't tolerate cowboys on my team."

Her eyes narrowed. "Is that what's going on here, *Agent Sandoval?*" Her voice dripped contempt. "You've finally found your reason to ditch me?" She closed the distance between them and stabbed a finger in his chest. "I heard you and Doc today. Any excuse would work, wouldn't it?"

He didn't respond.

"Wouldn't it?" Her voice rose. She shoved, open palmed.

Her eyes were bright with tears, her magnificent hair a wild gypsy nimbus around that face that wouldn't stop haunting him. Her chest heaved with emotion, tender flesh barely covered with fabric torn by a brute who had no right—

He grabbed the hand burning into his skin, his control teetering on the naked, ragged edge of yanking her close—

No. By the slimmest of margins, he seized hold of himself. Barely...barely he leashed the beast snarling to break free.

Grain by painstaking grain, he rebuilt the wall of his detachment until he dared speak.

He skinned his shirt over his head and handed it to her. "Go home, Jade." His voice was barely a whisper. "Now."

He flipped on his unit. "Bob."

"Yeah?"

"Come pick up Butler." His eyes never left hers, so wide and confused, as he gave Bob directions to their location.

"Be there in two minutes."

It was three.

Not that he was counting.

Chapter Nine

Jade paced her living room, too knotted up inside to sleep. Major's eyes followed her every step as he uttered an occasional whine of concern.

She couldn't find comfort in him right now. Like an automaton, she'd fed and watered him, given him the expected rubdown, but her heart wasn't in it.

Having more sense than people, Major didn't push her.

Unlike someone she was trying very hard not to think about. She wrapped her arms around her middle and fought the urge to scream.

Damn him. Damn him to hell. He wasn't going to rest until he had what he wanted: her off the team, tucked away in some sheltered corner.

She'd been on top of it. That guy was no threat to her, not really. Even if he'd been sober, she could have taken him, but no—Mr. Hotshot FBI Agent had to step in like some white knight, as if she were a helpless maiden.

She picked up the nearest object—a stupid little doodad she'd had some ridiculous idea would look pretty on that table—and let fly. It shattered against the wall in a satisfying shower of fragments—

Major yelped from behind her.

Jade broke. Sank to the floor and wrapped her arms

around his neck, holding on for dear life.

And wept. For the future that was in ruins, for the past she'd tried so hard to bury. As the dog who was her only true friend nosed at her hair and licked her cheek, offering solace, Jade rocked and sobbed and ached.

When she found herself slipping lower to lie on the floor in defeat, though, some remnant of the girl who'd remade a life surfaced.

She shoved herself back to sitting, then to her feet. She glanced down to realize that she still wore the shirt of the man who was trying to wreck everything she'd fought so hard to create.

She stripped it off, overcome for a second by the scent of him that clung to the fabric. She balled up the shirt, to cast it to the floor, imagining the pleasure of stomping it.

But she paused in the act, aware that the satisfaction would only be momentary.

She'd rather mash it into his face. If he thought she would simply lie down and let him run over her, he'd do well to reconsider.

Feeling better than she had in hours, Jade strode to the phone and, with a quick conversation, had the information she wanted.

On her march to the front door, she paused, seeing the shards everywhere. "You're smarter than me," she said to Major, "but I'm not going to risk you getting hurt." She delayed long enough to clear the mess, then gave Major a long, grateful hug.

"If only men were as dependable as dogs," she muttered. "I'll be back soon, fella."

T-shirt in her hand, she got in her car and left.

She located the house without any trouble, but sat outside for a minute, absorbing the shock. This was her dream house, the neat little cottage with pretty shutters and lots of windows, a tree-shaded lawn and—oh, man—a picket fence.

And her nemesis lived here.

Her opinion of him took a hit then, but she refused to feel it. Where he lived didn't matter.

What he intended to do to her dreams did.

She thought she would have knocked anyway, even if the whole house had been dark, but fortunately, she could see lights on in the back. She grasped the shiny brass knocker on the gleaming red door and rapped it hard, twice.

When there was no answer, she winced, conscious of the neighboring houses all closed down for the night, and rapped again but not quite so vigorously.

In the middle of the third effort, the door swung open.

Revealing a man she'd never met. Bare-chested, bare feet, hair tumbling over his brow, he had the same features as the one she knew, but the near-violent emotions crowding this man's face—

It was Alex, but it wasn't.

And in his hand, he held a paintbrush. Not one for covering walls but one for creating art.

He still hadn't said a word to her, though the air around them tumbled with a nasty mess of emotions that weren't all hers.

"Here—" She shoved the shirt at him, at a loss to recall what she'd thought to accomplish by coming.

His eyes, now dark as the shadowy floor of a forest, met hers. He made no move to take the garment.

She'd come here to fight, but now she didn't know how to proceed. What to think. How to deal with the man who loomed larger than ever before in a manner she didn't understand.

Finally, he raked his empty hand through his hair, then extended it to clasp the fabric in her fingers. With his elbow, he started closing the door.

"Wait—" She jammed her shoulder against the wood. "We need to talk."

"No." His head rose sharply. "No, we definitely do not need to talk. Not tonight."

He was probably right. Tempers were too frayed, bodies stretched on the fine edge of exhaustion. They had another hard day ahead, maybe many more.

But in his eyes she saw something she couldn't ignore, something that astonished her.

Loneliness as deep as her own.

So she merely feinted to the opposite side of the opening instead of pitting her strength against his, and slipped inside the door before he could stop her.

He hung his head and sighed. "Jade, it's been a long day."

She saw then the cost to him. He always appeared on top of things, so perfectly in control, calculating and unfeeling. Only when he'd spoken of his family had she glimpsed beneath that icy mask, at least until tonight, when his eyes had gone wild and savage. Even then, he'd clamped a lid on his emotions with inhuman quickness.

"Are you okay?" she blurted out.

She heard what might have been a snort. He shook his head and faced her. There was a knife scar on his left side just above the waist of his jeans. On his chest, she saw an old bullet wound.

A warrior, scarred and proud.

And troubled.

"Why are you here?" His voice was low and rough.

"I—" Suddenly, her mission seemed foolish. With his own blood, he'd earned the right to command.

She decided on honesty. "I don't know." She glanced at the floor. "I thought I did. I came here to duke it out, to force you to admit that you were being an asshole."

"I was."

Her head rose swiftly. "What?"

"You're right. I didn't blow cover, but if it had been Sean or Bob or anyone else but you—" He tossed the shirt aside. "I would have kept my distance."

She had no idea what to say.

"I guess that makes you happy." He turned away. "So you can go now." He stalked down the hall, calling over his shoulder, "Close the door behind you."

Under other circumstances, she might have done just that. Tossed a fist in the air and felt vindicated.

Might have—if she hadn't witnessed the tangle of misery in his eyes.

She closed the door, all right. Then she followed him.

And stopped mute at the threshold of the space he'd entered.

Two walls were mostly glass, with skylights in the ceiling. The room was beautiful, but that wasn't what held her immobile.

It was the paintings.

She could view only a fraction of them, stacked several deep everywhere as they were, but she'd never laid eyes on anything so stunning. Wild, vibrant color danced on the canvases, some of the images abstract and dangerous, some so real the faces seemed able to breathe, ready to speak.

She couldn't take it in quickly enough, this banquet, this

feast for the senses. Drama and power crackled through the room.

Finally, she found her voice. "These are amazing."

He whirled, and fury rode the air like thunder. "Get out of here." Frozen for only a second, he strode toward her, every line of his body filled with menace.

She was trespassing, she realized, on something very, very private. "I'm sorry, but—"

"Get out." He crowded her. Loomed over her, the force of his rage making her feel small.

But not threatened. He wouldn't hurt her.

She could hurt him, though, she recognized with a shock.

With a gesture that mimicked her earlier behavior only in form, she spread one hand against his chest, but slowly. Carefully, over his heart. "No."

His entire frame vibrated with the force of his emotions. He opened his mouth but nothing came out.

His eyes, though, spoke volumes. Temper. Violation.

Pain.

She didn't have the right words, only the certainty that she couldn't walk away, not yet. So she lifted the other hand and spread it against his heated skin with the impulse to protect the man inside.

His eyes, drowning dark, slammed shut as if the anguish was too great. Beneath her fingers, she felt as much as heard the rumble of a groan.

"I'm sorry," she murmured. Lifting herself to tiptoe, she placed her lips on his.

"Don't—" he protested.

But she felt a tremor rock his body.

Alex Sandoval had been many things to her, first a hero, then an adversary, but always larger than life, ever a figure of mystery.

But he was human, she grasped fully now. Vulnerable.

To her.

Incredible to understand that she had her own power to wield with him. The temptation of it beckoned, luring her toward something she didn't fathom yet but knew was important. Necessary in a way a primitive, buried part of her sensed.

It had nothing to do with logic, and everything to do with need.

Jade slid her arms upward. Her breasts made breath-stealing contact with his hard torso, and suddenly, she comprehended exactly the nature of the tension that crackled between them every second they were together.

When his mouth softened against hers, Jade smiled with satisfaction…and a healthy dose of fear.

And the shaky wall Alex had been building for hours—

Collapsed beneath the weight of one tender kiss.

His arms closed around her, and he couldn't let go.

Wouldn't.

Warring with himself more than her had sapped even his legendary control. He was wrong and she was right. He was too old and she too young. The weight of his guilt, the knowledge that he was burned out while she was bright as a new penny—none of it seemed to mean a damn when he was faced with this need for her. This hunger for so much more than the lush, ripe body that yielded against him as if she craved the closeness, too.

He took her mouth, fighting to keep from savaging her.

She fisted her hands in his hair and pushed him to the edge once more, daring him to tip over.

He tried to tear himself away.

She whimpered and held.

"Jade—" He gasped her name. Struggled to back off. "We

can't do this."

For a response, she scraped her teeth against his throat.

Dear God. Would she never stop challenging him? Never give him a minute's peace?

He got his answer when her hands slipped down his chest and tugged at the snap of his jeans.

Sweet mercy was his last coherent thought as she slid down his body and opened his fly.

"Not fast," he managed, sweeping her up and heading for his bed. "We are not doing this fast."

"Wanna bet?" With a husky laugh, she set her fingers and mouth to the task of driving him insane.

She held on to him and dragged him down to the mattress with her, contriving a quick reverse and rising to straddle him as she grasped the hem of her top and lifted.

"No." He stayed her hands. "Let me."

She smiled then, green eyes flaring with challenge. He peeled the cloth away slowly, rearing up to lick the salty dew from her skin, following the path of the fabric as it rose to unveil her in all her glory.

A Lorelei luring sailors to dash themselves on the rocks, auburn waves cascading over her shoulders and curling around the pale rose of her nipples.

"I didn't get it right," he murmured as he traced one ripe curve.

"What?" She threw her head back and dug her nails into his chest.

"Nothing." He barely felt the sting, caught in memorizing every line of her body, each swell and dip. He would try again to paint her and do her justice. He would fail. His skills were no match for the reality of her.

He clasped her hips, then her thighs, willing the denim away.

He readied himself to flip their positions and remedy the problem, but she bent to him first, secluding them behind the veil of her hair and shutting out the world.

He embraced her and let that world slip away, losing himself in the welcome of her kiss.

Jade slid down his body. When her breasts touched his naked chest, both of them groaned at the sudden lick of flame.

With shocking speed, she found herself on her back, his hands—oh, those hands, my God those hands—stripping her remaining clothes away as quickly as his own, then searching out as if by magic all the secret places that sent pleasure through her in slow, shimmering tendrils.

Erupting in bright streaks of lightning so sharp she cried out. "Let me," she sobbed with the pleasure, racing her hands over him as he conjured up a condom and sheathed himself. "Now, now—it has to be—"

One powerful thrust, and he was inside her.

Their eyes locked as each recognized the moment—

When everything trembled on the edge of change.

He held himself so still she could swear she heard both their hearts beat.

She couldn't speak.

Then, in his eyes, she saw him gathering one last attempt to keep her out.

She wrapped herself around him and held on. "Don't leave me," she said. "Please, Alex, don't leave."

He might have withstood the enchantress. Would have refused the demands of the rebellious cop. Somehow summoned the control to batter down his own screaming needs until they receded one more time.

But ignoring a plea from the woman who'd risen from a courageous young girl's devastation...

He was strong, but he wasn't that strong.

"Don't," she warned. "Don't you dare pity me. I'll hate you forever." She shoved at him and caught him off balance, then scrambled to the edge of the bed.

It would be smart for both of them if he let her go.

"I wish you could hate me," he said. "Or I could hate you." He rolled to his back. "Go home, Jade."

She bent to the floor and retrieved her top.

He studied each knob of her spine as the cotton rolled over it. Saw the defeat he'd put there, in her proud frame.

Hell with what was smart.

He lunged and caught her, tumbling her back to the mattress, pinning her with the weight of his body, trapping her slender wrists in his hands.

"Don't touch me." Her eyes spat sparks.

Consideration for women was ingrained in Alex at the deepest level. Both fathers revered the female of the species. He loosened his grip. "Get this straight, Jade. Pity isn't what I'm feeling right now."

Her eyes widened as he pulsed against her.

"You're a guy. You're not particular." She tried to shrug off any significance, temper still riding her.

But she wasn't afraid of him; that much was clear.

"I'm very choosy, as it so happens." He wanted to sink his teeth into that sulky lower lip.

"I don't know what to think of you." Reluctant humor battled with ire.

He shook his head with a rueful chuckle. "Join the club."

She squirmed beneath him, and he felt it ripple through his whole body.

"Stop that."

She did smile then, lifting an eyebrow in challenge. "And if I don't?"

"Damn it, Jade. You know we shouldn't—"

"Hush." She slipped her hands from his grasp and began to use them on him. "I've got your number now." She nipped at his jaw. "You're too old for me, right?"

One sizzling lick down his throat stalled his answer.

"Horse hockey." She trailed one hand over his back. "You're not really my boss, so you can't use that as an excuse. We're not breaking any rules."

He opened his mouth to argue, even though she was technically correct.

But her other hand slipped between them, and he lost his train of thought.

And that was before she wrapped her fingers around him.

Smiling with all the wicked, innate sensuality of her biblical namesake. "So…give me another reason." She moistened her lips.

Behind the sassy siren, though, he spotted nerves. The mix hit him where he couldn't resist.

"You won't make me sorry for this," he growled, and dug his hands into the sinfully rich mass of her hair.

"I wouldn't dare." She locked her arms around his neck.

"Of course you would." He took her mouth then, barely controlling the savagery of endless days of battling both himself and her.

She plucked at the hasty binding of his restraint and snapped it like so much string.

And did her own plundering. "If you stop, I'll have to hurt you."

"No way—" he gasped. "Open for me," he demanded as he yanked the cotton up and over her head.

She did more. Slid her hands down his back, over—

He thrust inside.

And there it was again. That moment, that foretaste of

everything altered, shifted.

Forever changed.

Her eyes caught his. Glanced away.

He could have dragged her back to face this, but he wasn't any more ready than she was.

Then she locked her legs around his hips in demand and banished all power of thought.

The first time should be slow and sweet, he'd always believed. Thorough and patient.

There was nothing of restraint in either of them. When he attempted to find his, to slow things down, Jade blocked him. Conquered him. Cast off his conscience as she battled, gave as good as she got.

He fought his release, grappled once more for the frayed threads of his discipline—

Until she arched beneath him. And screamed.

Magnificent. She was incredible, amazing. So strong. So sweet.

Alex roused her to climb once more, using every weapon at his disposal. "Again," he demanded, not sure how much longer he could hang on.

"I can't—"

"You can. You will." He felt it then, that ripple within her rising like a shockwave. When she flew apart this time, with a groan torn from his depths, he let himself soar with her.

Chapter Ten

Jade woke into darkness, not sure where she was at first.

Then registered the arm slung across her stomach, the body beside her.

Remembered.

And shivered.

Smiled. Wow. Double wow.

She swiveled her head toward him. Studied his face, enjoying the luxury of the time to do so without fear of being caught.

And barely resisted a sigh. He had a savage beauty that was all male, bold and powerful, even relaxed in slumber. His guard was dropped, exposing a vulnerability she imagined few had ever seen.

Then he stirred.

She held very still, realizing that she wasn't ready to confront what had passed between them.

Passed, hell. Detonated was more like it.

When Alex rolled to his side, away from her, Jade exhaled in relief. Her experience with the opposite sex wasn't that extensive. She'd been too focused on her goals to engage in serious relationships. She'd had sex, sure, but her life was her job, and that was all she needed for now.

At least, that was what she'd believed.

Until tonight.

Until…Alex.

She still reverberated with after-impressions of his mouth, his hands, the sheer power of him, so dark and…sumptuous. Lavish. As rich and ripe as his paintings.

She couldn't lie there any longer, this close to him. Her fingers itched to dive into his flesh, explore that amazing body again. See if what she recalled was for real or only imagination.

Her gaze trailed down the muscled planes of his back, and she considered rousing him from sleep in a manner that he'd probably enjoy. A lot.

And she might like too much. She wasn't prepared to find out that the deeper sense she'd had—one that went far beyond physical pleasure and into realms she'd thought the province of romance novels—could happen again with him.

Nope, not nearly ready for that.

So she slipped from his bed in the darkness, careful not to wake him. She gathered clothing—not sure how much was hers or his—and tiptoed from the bedroom.

In the hall, she sought out the bathroom, then closed the door carefully before turning on a light.

Only to discover that she'd retrieved his jeans and her torn tank top. In the mirror, though, she caught sight of a robe hanging on a hook behind her.

She donned it and was immediately surrounded by a spicy, mysterious scent she couldn't describe but only knew as Alex's. Swathed in fabric that had last touched his flesh, enveloped by the smell of him, Jade had to repress another shiver.

A delicious, treacherous one.

She flipped off the light and readied herself to return to his room to search for her jeans and shoes. As she crept down the hall, a spill of light from his studio beckoned.

When her hand touched the door frame, she halted, remembering his reaction when she'd followed him before. He was an intensely private man. She wondered if anyone else knew about this surprising talent of his.

His family, surely. The man who'd spoken of them with such love would paint for them, not hide it. But had Doc seen his work? His fellow agents?

Somehow she thought not, which inclined her even less to trespass, though her fingers tightened on the door frame with a powerful urge to see what was on the canvas he'd so hastily ripped from the easel.

"I applaud your restraint."

Jade whipped around at the sound of his voice. "I thought you were sleeping."

He cocked his head, his eyes dark and intense. "And still you didn't invade." He'd slipped on a pair of sweatpants, but his chest and feet were bare.

She didn't have to see the rest of the body hidden beneath the fleece. She would not soon forget it.

She decided on honesty. "But I want to."

A smile flickered briefly. "You puzzle me, Jade." His eyes locked on hers. "I can't resist solving a mystery."

She couldn't seem to catch her breath. "That's why you're a good detective, I guess."

He stared at her for a long time, then opened his mouth as if he had something important to impart.

Then he shook his head and shoved away from the wall. "Come on." He held out a hand.

She hesitated. "Where?"

The hand lowered, and she had a sense of him closing up. Shuttering the last trace of emotion from her view.

"In there." He gestured behind her.

His studio.

"No." She frowned. "I don't think—no."

He goggled, then the mask slid over his face again. "Why not?" His voice sounded indifferent.

His eyes were anything but.

"I barged into your house. You wouldn't let me see if I hadn't. We don't know each other well enough."

One eyebrow cocked. His head inclined toward the bedroom. "I'd say we know each other pretty intimately."

"Only physically," she said.

A flare ignited, quickly smothered. He performed an elegant shrug. "So you don't want to look anymore?"

"I—" She tore her gaze away with effort. "Of course I do, but you should have the choice. Is anyone else but your family aware that you have such talent?"

"Do I?"

"Don't be falsely modest. You're incredibly good."

"An art critic, are you?"

"Why are you acting this way?" At his stare of incomprehension, she expanded. "Pretending your art isn't important. What's the reason that all those paintings are stacked around the room instead of in a gallery? How come none of them are here on your walls?"

"My work is private." He stepped around her and continued into the studio, leaving her to choose whether to follow.

"Damn it, Alex." She stood outside the door and refused to look in. "I'm trying to be considerate."

His head popped around the corner, amusement dancing over his features. "Don't strain anything."

She grabbed his shoulder. "What are we doing?"

Seeing her own bewilderment reflected in his gaze settled her a little. "Beats the hell out of me."

She smiled at the absurdity of it all, and felt him relax under her hand. "Okay, I want to go inside—bad. Invite me again. Please."

"There's not much to look at, but—" Unease did a little tap dance behind his expression.

She squeezed his shoulder, both touched and afraid. "I don't understand the first thing about art, but what I glimpsed earlier knocked my socks off."

He grimaced and moved back. "Come on." But he stayed where he was, the shutters slamming back down.

Once inside, though, she lost the ability to focus on him, dazzled by the bounty that lay scattered all around the room.

Color exploded, each canvas unique—most in rich jewel tones, a few in cool pastels. Emotions covered the whole spectrum. Sorrow. Anger. Laughter. Love.

Yearning.

It was as if the man who lived under such ruthless control could only let himself feel here. Only dared let loose away from everything.

Everyone.

That touched her most, the loneliness singing through every brush stroke.

And pain that moved her to tears.

She sank to her knees in front of one, an old woman whose face was lined and worn but so luminous she might have been a saint. "Who is she?"

He didn't answer, and Jade dragged her gaze away in search of him.

He stared back, his mask stripped, revealing not a man who felt nothing.

But a man who felt far too much.

"How can you do this? Be a cop and see what you see? How can you stand it?" she whispered.

He studied her with eyes gone to dark, endless pools.

Without a word, he left the room.

Alex retreated into the kitchen, retrieving coffee beans and the grinder to buy time. Distance.

She tangled him up. He'd been so clear, once, on where they stood. Had to stand.

He snorted. To lie inside the privacy of his own thoughts was ridiculous. He'd never managed clarity where Jade Butler was concerned, not then and certainly not now.

"I'm sorry." Her voice came from the doorway, stiff and miserable. "If you could loan me a shirt, I'll be gone in just a second. I'll wash it and get it back to you, I promise."

He shook his head, arms braced on the counter. "No."

She said nothing for a minute, then continued in a small, bewildered tone. "All right, then. I'll just—"

He revolved, seeing her already retreating, the lapels of his robe gripped in one slim hand. "Jade, don't give me this kind of power. I don't want it." He stalked toward her, the turmoil inside him rising. Choking.

To her credit, she stood her ground, chin lifted, challenge sparking in those green eyes.

God, she was magnificent. Barefoot, freckles dusting her nose, garbed in a too-large robe falling from one shoulder, hair cascading untamed, she made something squeeze tight in his chest.

"You take my breath away."

Shock stumbled in her eyes. "What?"

And just like that, her honest confusion demolished his fury. The anger had only been displaced onto her, anyway, it dawned on him. There was a better target in this room.

And he was supposed to be a better man than this. He took advantage of her imbalance and tugged her hand from the lapel of his robe. "The apology should be mine." He pressed a kiss to her fingers and had the pleasure of seeing her pupils darken.

"I'll give you a shirt." From somewhere he found a faint smile. "Later." He drew her toward him. "I'm sorry, Jade. My painting is—" He shook his head, at a loss to describe how crucial his art was to him. It wasn't a matter for words.

"Private," she said. "Essential."

His gaze flicked to hers, then away.

She placed her free hand on his cheek. "I won't make you talk about it, Alex, but I just have to say one more thing about your work." When he tried to dislodge her hand, she refused. "It's stunning, the power of it, the beauty."

His chest felt tight. He wanted to hunch his shoulders, make her stop even as he drank in the praise.

"Let me finish." Her eyes never left him, and finally, he lifted his. "You have an amazing talent that should be exhibited. I won't lie and say I don't want to see more and to ask a million questions." She paused. "But I won't. Not until you're ready." A smile played over her lips. "Even though I'm dying to see the one you whipped off that easel earlier."

Not likely, he thought, and stepped back but bumped into the ell of the counter. He didn't want to discuss this. Wished she'd stop.

She moved to cage him in. "Okay. I get the message. I haven't earned the right to more, and maybe I never will, but—"

His mouth muffled her words as he chose the simplest method to shut her up.

Except that he got caught in the crossfire as desire shot like a flamethrower, searing them both.

"I want my hands on you." In a flash, he parted the robe, skimming them over the lush, ripe curve of her. He held the panels open and looked, just looked.

When she tried to shove them back, he blessed his greater strength. "No. Let me see you in the light. Sweet mercy—" With effort, he dragged his gaze up to hers.

And saw the bloom of furious color on her cheeks. "I should lose some—" She jerked the robe from his hands and whirled. "Don't."

He was always stepping wrong with her, but he couldn't leave her thinking that anything was flawed in how she was built. He closed the gap between them and spoke to her back. "Jade, you have a woman's figure. Maybe women today think boyish hips are ideal, but I promise you that no red-blooded man does."

Her shoulders had rounded, her fists clasping the robe at her throat. He risked placing one hand on her back, relieved when she didn't shrug him off. He heard the soft huff of breath and felt her relax a little, so he slid his hands into the waterfall of her hair and pulled her head back, exposing the pure line of her throat.

And sent his tongue on a long, slow slide down the feast of it.

Her knees buckled, and Alex grabbed the advantage. Turned her to face him and grasped her waist, then lifted her to the counter as he treated himself to the feast that was her mouth.

Jade swore her eyes rolled back in her head as he drew out the torture, trailing temptation with maddening leisure down her body. She arched under the sheer bliss of it, catching herself on her elbows, head thrown back as ecstasy beckoned.

Lips, tongue. Teeth, warm breath…and always, always, those unbelievably skilled artist's hands, painting desire on her in rich reds, tinting with cool blue reverence, smudging the shadows with wickedness in shades of raw sienna and burnt umber.

A kiss at the curve of a hip, then a glissade over the bone. Across the crease. Down.

Jade gasped and dug her fingers into his hair. Yanked. "Oh—You have to stop—"

His head rose, and dangerous lights glinted in his eyes. "I don't think you mean that."

He was right, she granted. That grin. Oh, that grin. Carnal and…playful?

He bent to her once more, and she caught her lower lip in her teeth as he sent her teetering to the edge—

And over, every nerve ending screaming as she soared, weightless.

He straightened, hands on either side of her, and watched her splayed across the tile.

"As soon as I find a muscle or two, you're toast," she warned.

No buccaneer ever smiled triumph more smugly. For once, no sorrow hovered in his eyes. "I can wait." He crossed his arms over his chest.

She found the strength. Reared, locking her legs around his waist, her mouth seeking his. "I can't."

He recovered quickly, sliding her hips to the edge, poised and ready.

Then growled. "Nothing in here," he muttered. "Hang on."

"What?" Before she could focus, he swung her off the counter and carried her from the room.

"Nightstand," he mumbled. In several long strides, he'd covered the distance and tumbled her onto the mattress, then rummaged in the top drawer.

When he turned to her, his eyes were a simmering dark caramel.

She held out a palm for the packet. "Let me."

"Keep your distance." A corner of his mouth quirked. "I'm not finished with you. Touch me now, and I can't promise what will happen."

While his attention was diverted, she fought dirty, hooking a foot around his leg, toppling him to the mattress. She rose over him, flicked her hair behind one shoulder and cracked her joined fingers as if she were a virtuoso ready to demonstrate her skill on the keys. "I'm touching you. Try and stop me."

Alex endured the onslaught—barely. Straddling him, the wet, warm heat of her taunting, Jade used every weapon in her impressive arsenal, firing shot after shot without quarter. A nip here, a stroke there, the fan of her thick, silken hair over flesh driven to goose bumps. And everywhere—oh, sweet mercy—everywhere that delicious, murderous mouth.

And laughter, free and easy, until she teased it from him, too.

He'd never made love with laughter as the harmony note tripping over and around the melody that was desire.

Finally, he'd had enough—no, never enough, he realized. With a pang, he understood that he'd never get his fill of this. Of her.

But he couldn't—wouldn't—risk even one more night. Not while her life was on the line. In his hands.

And if he blew it, if anything happened—

He squeezed his eyes shut.

She faltered, perhaps sensing his turmoil. "Alex? What's wrong? Did I do something—"

He reared up, kissed her hard. Put his mind to soothing hers, pulling from somewhere a reassuring grin. "You did a lot of somethings," he murmured as his tongue traced just below her ear.

Then he flipped them. "Tag—you're it." He lowered his head so she couldn't see his eyes. When he nuzzled at her rib cage and she giggled, he forcibly cast the worries out of his mind and focused on her pleasure.

If this was to be their one night together until this operation ended, he would make the hours ones neither would forget.

And when tomorrow came, he would redouble his efforts to keep her safe.

For, beyond the bounds of all good sense, he was well and truly hooked on Jade Butler. This might be the last reverie for a while, but he would use every skill honed over a long career to make sure there could be others.

And pray that, this time, his best would be sufficient to shield her from harm.

Chapter Eleven

Morning light filtered in. Delight danced on the breeze through the open window behind the bed. Jade stretched, and well-being echoed throughout every replete inch of her.

Alex's bed, that's where she was, where she wouldn't mind staying for the next century or so.

What a man. Whew—Alex Sandoval was some kind of lover. She smiled and turned her head to greet—

No one. He was gone.

She rolled over and brought his pillow into the curve of her body, inhaling the welcome scent of him. Wishing he were within reach, all that toned, tasty flesh, the electrifying power of him.

A shiver rippled through her. *Mamma mia.* If he were here, she'd be tempted to sink her teeth into him. Never let him out of this bed—

Wait. She sat up in shock, raking her hair back. What time was it?

Seven a.m. She'd had—they'd had—about an hour of sleep, but that couldn't matter now. Major needed feeding and she had to change before work. She hopped on one foot as she pulled on jeans, searched for shoes.

Her top, she recalled all too well, wasn't fit to cover a

soup can, much less her chest. "Alex, may I borrow a shirt?"

Only silence greeted her. "Alex?"

No water running in the shower. She grabbed the robe he'd torn off her last night and wrapped it around her before she headed down the hall to investigate. As she passed his studio, she noticed that the door was closed. She paused and raised her hand to knock. "Alex?"

The house felt empty. Instead of knocking, she put her hand on the knob but didn't turn it.

She backed away without opening the door. She would honor her promise to respect his privacy.

In the kitchen, a folded note was propped on the counter next to a pot of coffee, already made. She smiled at his thoughtfulness. She'd kill for a cup, though she thought she might just float through the day on the tide of outrageous contentment that suffused her. She reached for a mug while perusing her name on the outside of the paper in bold, sweeping letters that suited the artist as much as the cop. She poured coffee with one hand while opening the paper with the other.

Jade—

I have an early appointment. There are T-shirts in the second drawer of the chest—take your pick. I owe you one.

She smiled, remembering him peeling hers off, and tasted a sip.

Good coffee, Agent Hunk. She saluted with the mug and flipped the note to its back to continue.

And frowned as she read.

Team meets at eleven. Sandoval.

Sandoval? That was it? She stared as though she might find more written in invisible ink or something. As she peered, she noted, beneath the *Sandoval*, strokes that would have formed an A.

He'd started to sign his first name, then changed his mind.

Her mug cracked on the counter.

Anger tried to swim up through the sea of hurt. After what they'd shared last night, he was placing distance between them as fast as he could travel.

Why, Alex? Didn't you see how it was between us?

She felt sick. Cheap. Stupid.

And at last, fury rode to the rescue, shoving its way past heartache.

Jade stomped from the sunny kitchen that had become far too cheery for her mood. She cast his robe to the floor and yanked open the second drawer of his chest, jerked the top shirt off the pile—

And just as quickly jammed it back. She'd wear that tank top home. Be damned if she'd take anything from him.

She was about to rage her way out the front door when it hit her that leaving signs of her temper would only hand him more ammunition. If he could be this callous after—

She wouldn't think about the night, not ever again.

Sure thing, Jade. She'd remember this experience for the rest of her life.

But she'd make it an object lesson.

She swallowed her hurt and outrage and forced herself back into the bedroom, where she made the bed with precision, smoothing away every last bit of evidence of the hours they'd spent gorging on pleasure. She even retrieved the condom wrappers from the floor, to be cast in the first neutral-site trash can she encountered.

The robe was returned to its hook, the mug rinsed and placed back on the shelf, the coffeepot turned off and washed.

The note—

She resisted the urge to tear it into confetti.

Instead, she'd take it with her as reinforcement, lest she be tempted to falter in her resolve.

At the doorway, she paused and looked around the little house that could have been torn from the scrapbook of her dreams. When a pang of longing for what might have been arrowed its way into her heart, she ruthlessly plucked it out.

The last traces of her girlhood hero worship vanished right along with the foolish fancies of a woman who had never allowed herself a mistake of this magnitude.

She had less than four hours to get her emotions squared away and get back on the job.

That was all that had been important for a long time, all that could matter now, the job. She was a cop and a damn good one. It was the female who was on shaky ground.

So she'd be a cop. And she'd show Alex Sandoval.

Jade arrived well in advance of the meeting. Alex heard her voice and had cause to consider, yet again, how else he might have handled the morning.

Maybe he would have found a better way if he hadn't been so snarled up by her, by the magic and power of the night. Still was, for that matter. He'd slapped a strip of masking tape over the gaping hole where his legendary control had gone missing, but the tape was straining at the edges.

He should go see her, ask her to step into his office and explain, clearly and calmly, why a repeat of last night would have to wait. She was a good cop; she'd understand.

And if she was shaken half as badly as he was, she might

even welcome the respite.

Oh, yeah. Sure. He couldn't even sell that line to himself.

Even now, he wanted his hands on her so badly he'd chew through razor wire to get to her.

Which was exactly why he had to keep his distance.

Just then, her laughter drifted from the bullpen as she and Sean traded quips. She didn't sound upset. That was good; she probably had reached the same conclusion about sensible behavior.

Why wasn't she upset, damn it?

"Hey, Alex," Bob called out from behind him. "Got some results on the ligature for you."

Alex lowered his head and braced his arm against the wall as he struggled past the urge to ignore Bob and grab Jade.

"Great," he forced himself to say. "Come on in."

With effort, Alex moved to his desk and sat in his chair. The sooner they wrapped up the case, the sooner he could find a way out of this labyrinth.

Two hours later, Jade strode into the meeting beside Bob, a smile on her face. "Yeah, yeah, yeah. Your wife is going to buy that a bass boat is a sign of your enduring love for her."

Bob's face creased in mock outrage. "She can come with me. Time for companionship and simple pleasures." He made his appeal to the room. "Isn't that what marriage is all about?"

"I thought it was free sex," Sean chimed in.

Jade snickered. "How do you ever get laid, Sean?"

Banter ensued. Alex let it go on for a minute, knowing they'd all been putting in a lot of hours on this case. He sat very still and kept his eyes on the notes he'd been assembling.

Until Jade's husky laughter arrowed straight to his gut. How could she be so unaffected by what had passed between them last night?

He glanced up and caught her unaware.

And saw the misery behind what he realized now was forced humor.

He dropped his gaze and scrambled to regroup.

The case. Everything now had to be about wrapping it up. "Okay, people. Let's compare notes." He would seek refuge in procedure and shove emotion under a rock. "Bob, what's happening on the missing bouncer?"

"No airline or bus tickets sold to that name, but his neighbors haven't seen him in a few days. We're tracking any relatives to find out if he's visiting. He hasn't been in Austin but six months and, according to his fellow employees, seems to be a loner. Man of few words. No friends we can tap to track his movements around town. I'm waiting for credit card records to determine what we can learn about the mysterious Mr. Howard." His expression revealed his frustration.

Alex understood the feeling and granted Bob a diversion. "Tell them what you've got on similar crimes."

Bob launched into the explanation he'd shared with Alex earlier, and Alex listened with one ear, sifting information, shuffling it around as he'd learned worked best. Sometimes the conscious mind got too intent on a case, and patterns evaded notice.

"So the upshot is that the film angle is unusual. One case in New Jersey, one in L.A. with similarities, but the strings of celluloid element is missing in the L.A. case, and the Jersey perp is behind bars." Bob shrugged. "My gut says this is local."

"I concur," Alex said. "Marco, what have you got on the personnel of the second bar?"

"Owner's based in Dallas. Manager was cooperative. His story checks out, as do those of the other employees except one waitress and a busboy."

"Women aren't normally serial killers, but she could be an accomplice—any connection to the first bar or to Rick Howard?"

"Funny you should ask. Howard used to hang out there when he first got to town. I ordered a composite sketch obtained from the staff of Wild Child. We'll show it around at Night Dreams. Hope we get a hit."

"The clock's ticking, people. There's only one girl left. I don't want to be making a call to her parents." He glanced around the room, understanding that they were equally frustrated. "What about the busboy? He a possibility?"

"Can't say yet. I have a feeling he's illegal. Too many of them work the crap jobs around town, get paid cash on a day rate. Bars are a cash business, and it's easy to fudge records on everything but the liquor."

"Keep pushing."

"I will."

"Meanwhile, we continue to reach out to other sources, especially film related. On that note, Case, how are you coming on access to class rosters from UT?"

"Still doing the song and dance over privacy, but I'm angling for a sympathetic judge to issue a warrant. Expect to have it tomorrow, at the latest."

"What about membership in the film society?"

The assistant U.S. attorney rolled his eyes. "Folks in that industry get pretty rabid over freedom of speech. They're threatening to bring in the ACLU."

Alex saw the gleam, though. "But?"

"Nothing yet, but if I could snag some manpower to help, there's a film society membership meeting tonight, open to the public. Thought we could mingle. Snap a few pictures while we're at it."

"Good idea," Alex said.

"We're spread thin with the bars," Sean noted.

"No bars tonight." Alex waited for Jade's reaction.

It didn't take long.

"Why not?" she demanded.

"We're spinning our wheels. I don't have the budget for endless overtime with no results."

"We'll get results." Temper simmered.

"You can't force things, Butler." He met her furious gaze. *And I warned you what I'd do.*

"Sir." Her tone snapped challenge. "It's our best avenue."

If her eyes had been lasers, he would have had a smoking hole in his chest right now.

But the remainder of the team was far too interested in the pyrotechnics. He turned away, dismissing her. "What's the age range, you think, Case? How many can we credibly harvest from the team to put inside?"

"My investigator tells me that the majority are young—twenties, thirties—but there's a solid segment that's older, even into their sixties."

"So—" Alex scanned the group "—Sean, for sure, and Evan. Bob, if you can managed to douse those cop's eyes, you're in. Marco, give me that list of female uniforms. I'll pull a couple in—your choice." He paused, then looked at Jade. "Butler, I'm not fully comfortable with the risk of exposing your cover, but—"

"But it could go either way," she prompted. "I just might snag our guy's interest, if my hunch about the fame angle is on target." Her body language dared him to disagree.

He obliged her. "It removes a layer of protection for the undercover role."

"Sometimes there's no choice. We all know budgets are limited, and undercover cops often have to do double duty."

"It's not how I prefer to operate. I'm not convinced we're at that point yet." As she gathered herself to protest, he held up a hand to forestall her. "Dress the part, though you'll remain on the sidelines until we've had a chance to scope this out."

He could see that she wasn't fully satisfied, but she was wise enough to accept partial victory. "Okay. Next—we need to cover the results of the tire track fragment recovered at the second scene. Sean?" After that, he'd have someone check on the tox screen from the medical examiner.

He settled back in his chair to listen.

Beneath the radar of the group's attention, Jade cast a glance at him—

Whipping her head back when she saw him already watching her.

But not quickly enough to prevent him noticing the hurt he couldn't afford to soothe.

When the meeting broke up, Jade cut through a knot of people moving toward the door.

"Butler," said the voice she most didn't want to hear.

She continued into the hall. If she moved fast enough, she could claim not to have heard him.

"Hey, Jade," Sean hailed her. "Alex's asking for you."

Damn. "Tell him to give me a minute. I've got a call to make." She wasn't lying, exactly. She had a whole list of calls, even if they could wait.

She just wasn't ready to talk to him. She couldn't seem to

summon her game face, and she'd be damned if she would let him get to her any more than he already had. Her throat burned as she remembered the night, how she'd initiated contact, then shed every last inhibition with him. That he could walk away so easily ate at her unmercifully.

Ducking behind her desk, she seized upon the phone message lying there with the request that she contact Dan Fleming. When Alex strode out of the conference room seconds later, his expression thunderous, she waved the pink slip of paper and held up her finger to request a delay.

His eyes narrowed, but his expression remained otherwise blank. A curt nod was his only response.

Blowing out a sigh of relief, however unwarranted, she punched in Dan's number.

"Hey! Are you okay, Jade? I heard you had some trouble last night."

A brain-freezing second elapsed before she realized that he would be talking about the scene in the bar and not the night with Alex that had eclipsed everything before. "Yeah, well…some people can't accept no for an answer."

"But you're all right?"

He sounded so earnest and worried. "Yes, I'm fine. I've had worse happen."

"Your job is dangerous. I…worry about you."

She could practically hear the blush. "That's sweet, Dan." She needed to switch to business but didn't want to be rude.

"I wondered if—" He paused. "Never mind. Probably not your cup of tea. You might be busy with work, anyway."

"What?"

"I—well, there's this Austin Film League meeting and screening of a Sundance winner tonight, and I wondered if you'd, you know. Like to go with me."

She paused, struck by the possibilities. By the sheer pleasure of rubbing Alex's nose in an opportunity he planned to deny her.

"Never mind. I shouldn't have asked." Dan's voice made it clear that he'd put the wrong spin on her hesitation.

"No—no, that's not it. I mean, I'm not sure about tonight, but—could I check on our plans and get back to you?"

"Sure. No problem."

She heard the enthusiasm. *What a jerk I am, taking this guy for a ride.* She glanced toward Alex's office.

On the other hand, Alex obviously wasn't as affected as she'd been by the night's events.

Rapidly she tallied the pros and cons.

Pro: Dan would know people at the meeting. They wouldn't be suspicious of her when she was with him.

Con: He would recognize the rest of the team, so it was a risk to assume he could carry off the masquerade, though he hadn't done badly in the bar.

And the big negative: Alex would be furious with her for doing this behind his back.

No way was she going to jeopardize this case. She wouldn't proceed further with Dan until she conferred with Alex, but she'd do her best to make him see the advantages.

"Let me see how my day shakes out. All right if I touch base with you later?"

"You bet."

"Great. Now, you didn't call just to ask me out."

"No, not that it isn't a good enough reason." His voice held a smile. "I have something for you, I think."

"What?"

"A partial image I missed the first time through. It's part of a guy standing in what could be the second warehouse."

"Are you kidding me? When can I get it?" She frowned. "How come you're not already talking to Alex?"

"Because I figured if I handed you an advantage, you might have some incentive to move up the rain check you offered me."

"Dan, that's—"

"Sneaky? It is, isn't it?" He sounded delighted with himself.

She had to grin. Maybe this was what it was like to have a kid brother. "Can you email the image to me?"

"Email will lose too much resolution. I've got prints that are better."

"I'll be there in ten minutes to pick them up."

"I have an errand to run anyway. I was about to leave. I'll bring them to you."

"Great. Terrific." She played with the end of her braid. "Can I tell Alex before you get here?"

He laughed. "Sure."

"Wow—thanks, Dan. I owe you."

"Yeah. Yeah, you do." With a smile in his voice, he was gone.

Jade did a little Snoopy dance behind her desk.

Sean glanced sideways. "What's up?"

She turned a wide smile on him. "Me, by a point." She started toward Alex's office. "A big one."

So there, Sphinx. But she was too excited to hold a grudge.

Maybe he didn't want her, but he'd jump at this information, and if she worked it right, he'd have to let her in, front and center, on the operation tonight.

Alex was slow to answer her knock, still off balance about how to handle her. "Come in."

He didn't look up immediately, not until he was sure his expression was fully composed. He paused in the notes he was making. "Have a seat."

She fairly vibrated with excitement. "Guess what?" But she didn't wait for his answer. "Dan's got a partial image of someone who might be our guy."

Alex rounded his desk. "Where is it?"

"He's bringing it over. Be here in ten minutes."

He grabbed the phone. "Bob, where's that composite? Get me a copy in the next ten minutes." His blood was pumping. At last, a break.

Jade shifted. Suddenly, the room seemed too private, the silence between them too huge.

Somehow, he had to clear the air. "Jade—"

She spoke at the same time. "There's something—"

He halted, uncomfortable in the extreme. "Ladies first."

"No, you—" She gripped her hands. "Okay. Hear me out before you go ballistic."

Not an auspicious introduction. He forced himself to remain still. "I don't go ballistic."

"No. Of course you wouldn't." Her tone was clear that she intended no compliment. "Anyway, here's the deal. Dan invited me to the screening tonight. I'm go—" She shot him a glance. "I'd like to go."

Before he could object, she picked up speed. "It makes more sense. He knows people there and could introduce me to them. He's part of that crowd, so even if someone recognized me from the bar, they wouldn't be suspicious if I'm with him."

He said nothing, so she continued. "We don't want to risk him exhibiting surprise when he sees some of the team, but he won't if we warn him. It's a tailor-made opportunity to pose lots of questions, the way you do when you're on a first date, meeting the other person's friends."

First date. Dan asked me out.

She'd been in his bed last night, damn it. She was his, even if he couldn't claim her yet.

"I'm right, Alex. You know I am."

The hell of it was, he did. The chance was one they couldn't discard, and he had no choice but to ignore the primitive part of him that still wanted her safely shielded from harm.

Tucked in his bed. Held in his arms.

He was about to acknowledge her point when Bob walked in. "Here you go."

Everything else receded to second place as Alex bent to study the face on the paper. Shaggy blond hair nearly to the shoulders framed a thick neck and bulldog jaw.

"He looks like a bouncer," Jade murmured, her arm brushing Alex's as she pored over the sketch.

"Height?" Alex worked to ignore the familiar scent of cinnamon and peaches.

"Six-foot, six-one," Bob answered. "About two hundred twenty pounds."

High cheekbones, thin lips. Almond-shaped eyes. "Eye color?"

"Light is all anyone could recall. This guy didn't spend a lot of time with his fellow employees, but you'd think at least one of them would have noticed—" He chuffed in disgust.

"That's more than we've had. It's being distributed?"

Bob nodded. "All patrol units are getting it on their computers, and print copies will be handed out to each shift throughout APD. Every member agency of the task force will have one within the hour, as well. We're keeping a lid on it from the media. Don't want the guy running. What about tonight, Alex? Hit the clubs after all?"

"I'll decide in a few minutes. We may have a break. Fleming recovered an image that might be our guy. He'll be here with it any minute." Alex frowned. "Why didn't he send it electronically?" he asked Jade.

"He said it wasn't great and he wanted us to have the best resolution possible."

"Okay." An uncomfortable silence fell then. Alex cast her a glance.

She met it. Instantly evaded.

If Bob weren't there...

But he was. Just as well, anyhow. Any possible discussion would require much more than a few minutes. And privacy.

Even if he knew what the hell to say.

"Why's he doing this?" Jade puzzled. "Is it just for kicks? Some ax to grind?"

"Not for kicks," Alex answered. "This one's an organized killer. Nothing spur of the moment about the way the crime scene is posed. He likes control. He's of above average intelligence and has a lot of rage, but it's likely tucked away. He lost it with the first victim, but that was a fluke.

"People who know him would either say he has good social skills or that he kept to himself, but either way, they'll be surprised he's the one." He paused. "He's probably out there watching us, maybe even a little frustrated that he hasn't made the news as often as he'd like. Our keeping the lid on the coverage doesn't give him the satisfaction he's after."

"He's doing this for publicity?" Jade asked.

"No, not primarily, but he wants to be admired. First by these girls, then by the world for coming out on top. He's filmed them." Alex locked his eyes on her. "If he can get his hands on you, he'll put a camera on you, too. While he forces you to tell him how terrific he is, how strong he is. He'll torture you just as he's tortured them."

Mossy green eyes went dark, then hardened. "You want to scare me. You think I'm not aware that this is dangerous? You try getting into cars with johns, completely unarmed, clear that all one has to do is hit the gas and drive you to some dark field where all you have going for you is your hand-to-hand training, while you're hamstrung by a tight skirt and killer heels." The eyes were hollow-point bullets now. "I got this assignment not just because I know how to strut and attract attention, Agent Sandoval, but because I can keep my head even when I'm in danger."

He rose from the edge of his desk. Loomed over her to press his point further.

"Excuse me," Dan Fleming spoke from the doorway. "Sorry to interrupt. I thought you'd want to see this immediately."

"Don't mind them," Bob said. "Just a little *mano á mano* going on. We cops like to do that for entertainment." The glare he gave Alex was anything but complimentary.

Great. Just great. "What have you got?" Alex held out a hand.

Fleming glanced between Alex and Jade but was smart enough to keep his mouth shut. He lifted the flap of a brown envelope. "I wish it were more. I don't know how much it will help."

Alex accepted the photo and stifled his disappointment. Only the guy's shoulder. He reached back for the composite, but Jade beat him to it, handing him the sheet of paper they'd been studying.

She and Bob ranged on either side of him as they compared the two.

"Tough call," Bob said. "Sketch artist didn't attempt the physique. And the shoulder shot is from the back."

He sounded as disappointed as Alex felt.

"The lab in D.C. can do some impressive stuff. Let's see what their reaction is." Alex twisted to grab his phone.

"If I could have a look—" Fleming said. "I—in my spare time, I like to play around with different software. There's one I have that does morphing. I believe it could be adapted to combine these two and complete an image."

Alex hesitated. "Humans have infinite variations. We've all seen heads that don't seem to fit bodies."

"That's true, but—" Fleming halted.

"But what?"

"Notice the background. I really think it's him because the wall—" With a slight hesitation as if seeking permission, Fleming approached and pointed. "See that crack partway up? It matches one in a photo you sent me, taken at the first crime scene." He lifted his palms. "Sorry—I didn't bring my copies."

"Hold on a second." Alex rounded the desk and retrieved a stack of photos, then shuffled through them, squinting closely. "Here?" He frowned. "You sure of that?"

"Yes. I enlarged it for comparison."

Bob's eyebrows rose. "Well…we've had less to go on."

Alex nodded. "How soon could you finish the morphing?"

Fleming beamed. "Give me an hour. Two at most."

"Do it. Fleming—" Alex caught him before he made it to the door.

The younger man executed a turn. "Yes?"

"Jade tells me you've invited her to a screening." Deliberately, Alex encroached into the comfort zone, using his greater height to peer down his nose. "You're a bright fellow. I figure you've already tumbled to the possibility that our guy might have some connection to the movie business." Whether Rick Howard did remained to be seen.

Alex leaned forward, felt satisfaction that Fleming retreated a step. "That being the case, if you aren't positive you can play your part, speak up now. I wouldn't take it kindly—" his tone conveyed the strength of the threat "—if you do anything to jeopardize my detective's safety."

"Oh, no, sir." Fleming's eyes widened. His voice wavered, just a little. "I would never—I mean—" He shook his head. "I promise you I'll be very, very careful with her." He glanced at Jade, his gaze filled with longing. "Jade is, well..." He actually blushed. "What can I do to set your mind at ease?"

You can stay the hell away from Jade.

Good God. He was actually standing here in front of a fresh-faced kid, feeling jealous because Jade's body was tense beside him like some mama bear over her cub.

To her credit, though, she remained silent. He was certain she would have things to say later.

Mama bear, not girlfriend bear, he reminded himself. Though Fleming was near her age, not an old guy like him.

"I may want both, but do the photos first. Fleming—" He caught the kid as he turned to leave. "Jade will go with you tonight, assuming nothing else breaks in the case. Follow her lead to the letter, and if you see her backup, find a better poker face than what you've shown thus far."

Fleming's expression was sober. "I'll do my best." His gaze shifted to Jade. "Want me to pick you up, or—?"

She gifted him with a smile. "I'll meet you there. What time?"

"Alamo Drafthouse on Anderson. Doors open at seven, but I have to be there by six-thirty to set things up."

"I'll arrive at six-thirty, too, then."

"Great. Um—" He looked around the room. "I—I'll just get to work and call you as soon as I have something, Agent Sandoval."

"You do that." Alex gave Fleming his back. "That's it, everyone."

Bob left, Jade right behind him.

"Butler." She didn't slow. "Jade."

She paused. Stiffened. Finally…slowly…turned.

He wondered if the hurt in her eyes was as evident in his own. "About this morning—"

"This isn't the place," she said. "Or the time."

His shoulders settled. "Yeah." He glanced down at his desk without seeing. "But we need to talk."

Her nod was curt. "Maybe." She spun on her heels and departed.

Leaving Alex staring after her. Wishing he could rewind the day and start all over.

Chapter Twelve

Jade knocked on the glass doors of the locked theater. Inside, a brunette with black horn-rims glanced up from her post inside the concession stand and shook her head, pointing to her watch to indicate that Jade was too early.

Down, girl. Jade cautioned herself against the irritation of a busy cop. She managed a smile and mouthed the name *Dan Fleming.*

The girl's eyes went wide, then she frowned. *Dan?* She and the boy beside her exchanged incredulous expressions. *A woman here for Dan?* the young man asked.

On Dan's behalf, Jade was incensed. He was a decent guy and attractive. Yes, he was a bit nerdy and shy, but these two wouldn't win any prizes, either.

She rapped again, twice. Hard.

The girl threw up her hands and headed Jade's direction. She unlocked the door and pushed it forward. "We're not open yet. Dan's—"

Just then, Dan rushed through an door on the far side of the lobby. "Jade—sorry. I had some trouble with the projector." His eyes darted between her and the girl, and despite his assurances to Alex, he was much too flustered to be an asset.

Jade took over. "Hi, Dan. It's so sweet of you to invite me." She put a little of a simper into the smile she cast the girl. "Isn't he just the greatest? I was so flattered that he'd let me come watch him at work." She flipped her hair over one shoulder. "I find the film business absolutely fascinating, and Dan's so patient with teaching me about it."

She hadn't been sure exactly how to play it, but she'd had a sense that, given her lack of the terminology, she'd do better to play this as starstruck and eager, a little bit vain. A touch of the airhead would help in making people take her lightly and considering her unthreatening.

It seemed to be working. "Yeah, whatever," the brunette said. "I've got to get back."

"I'm Jade, by the way." Jade stuck her hand out.

"Cicely." The handshake was returned without enthusiasm.

"Thanks, Cicely. I'm sorry to interrupt your busy evening. Have you been doing this long?"

"Four years." Cicely granted her a faint smile. "I started as soon as I enrolled in my first-semester film classes."

"Cicely's the president of the film league," Dan said. "She keeps all of us on our toes."

I'll bet she does, Jade thought. Cicely would bear cultivating.

But she wouldn't push now. "That's impressive. Maybe I could ask you some questions later, when you're not so busy, you know?"

"Yeah, maybe." Cicely stalked back to the concession stand.

"I'm sorry," Dan murmured. "She's not the friendly sort, but the league would collapse without her—" He broke off. "I didn't mean to be late coming down."

Jade heard the nerves. "Easy. You're doing fine." She squeezed his arm and kept her voice low. "Introduce me to people whenever it's appropriate for your normal behavior. Just go on with whatever you'd usually do, and I'll tag along.

If I need to break away, I will."

"Okay." He exhaled. "All right. I—it's obvious I'm a filmmaker, not an actor, I guess."

"Don't sweat it. I'll do the acting."

He led her across the lobby and introduced her to the other two people whose paths they crossed. On the stairs to the projection booth, he stopped. "You're good at this. They're really buying the airhead routine. You'd be an excellent actress. Do you like this part of your job?"

She narrowed her gaze and hissed. "Is there anyone up those stairs?"

"Up—?" His eyes widened. "Oh, God. I didn't think. No," he hastened to add. "There's no one. Man, I am really not suited for this, am I?"

"Forget it. Just keep cool. Discussions later." When he seemed so chastened, she relented and smiled. "Acting, huh? So maybe I've missed my calling?"

He relaxed. "Could be."

As she followed him up the stairs, she pondered the novel concept of herself in film. She thought of undercover work as selling the role, but always in the larger context of catching criminals. Would she wish to be in the movies?

Nah—she'd always wanted to be a cop. And this part of it was seldom all that much fun. Unlike someone onstage or in front of a camera, her screwups could have far more serious consequences than a blow to her ego. They could get her—and maybe others—killed.

At the top of the stairs, she scanned the booth while her eyes adjusted to the dim light. Automatically, she sought out hiding places and potential dangers. Aloud, she began to describe the setup for the benefit of those listening in the parking lot. "Not a lot of room here, is there? Only this one access?"

She led Dan through his paces, filing away the information, though the likelihood of any activity was low. She was mostly here to ferret out potential suspects.

When Dan's recitation wound down, she nodded toward the door. "Okay—enough time up here. Do you have to stay until the show starts?"

He shrugged. "Mostly I do, but sometimes I go back down and hang out. We're always shorthanded."

"Let's do it, then. I'll make myself useful. With luck, no one will mind if I remain and mingle when you have to come back up here."

"What if it doesn't work? Cicely's kinda territorial."

"Leave Cicely to me. And just think of this as improv theater." She smiled. "I'm pretty good at switching directions on the fly."

His answering grin was wide. "You fascinate me, Jade. This doesn't count as our rain check, right?"

She chuckled and patted his shoulder. "Nope. Now—back to work." She paused. "And thanks for this, Dan. You're a sweet guy."

Despite the dim light, she could see the color rise to his cheeks.

They might be only a year apart in age, but decades separated them when it came to life experience.

You fascinate me, Jade. Bob rolled his eyes at Alex, and Alex grimaced. If he had his choice, there'd be no rain check for Jade and the puppy.

He'd decided to split the team to run both operations tonight. Some of them could pull double duty, since the club scene got started much later. Another female officer would work the Sixth Street district this time. Alex had dropped by to follow this one for a while.

"Butler as bimbo," Bob remarked. "Never would have guessed she could be so convincing, intense and driven as she is."

Alex only grunted. He'd managed to bury the worst of the turmoil inside him, but maintaining his usual distance wasn't easy. Jade's point, made somewhere along the way when he'd been half out of his mind and lost in her body, was strictly true: he was not in her direct line of command, so they'd broken no regulations, not even unofficial taboos. Cops got involved with other cops all the time.

But he'd shot his objectivity all to hell, and he was having a tough time getting it back.

"Maybe it would have been more profitable for us to keep Fleming working on that morphing program. This is a long shot."

Bob's eyebrows lifted. "How many homicides have you investigated, Alex? Think you can even count them all?"

Alex shrugged. "Not without a calculator."

"You have the experience to know this is the hard part, when you only have pieces and none of them fall into place. Not enough to construct the theory that does the *ka-ching* sound when your gut says you're on the right path. It's easier then, when you sense what's happened and can set about proving it. Right now, you're just tugging at loose threads in a variety of scenarios to see what's solid and what will unravel."

"Yeah." Alex rubbed his forehead. Sometimes he thought he'd been tired for years. "It's just—" He let his hand drop. "Nothing." No purpose would be served by thinking about anything but the case.

"You could have had thirty days off when you transferred," Bob noted. "But instead you take a weekend, then jump right into work here. You'd handled that backbreaker sniper case right on top of the guy who held the whole nursery school hostage for nearly three days. Ask me, you should be clocking some vacation time the minute we wrap this one up."

"I didn't." Alex's jaw locked. "Ask, that is." He relented. "Appreciate the concern, Bob, but I'm fine."

"Just tell me this. How many weeks of unused leave do you have stored up?"

"I had to take nearly a week when Liam got hurt."

Hall snorted. "That doesn't count as vacation—conducting a manhunt for Liam's lady, staving off the press and all those fans holding vigil." He held up his palms. "You're not listening, but you should. You're walking a fine line, Alex. Don't know a better agent than you, not even Doc, but that doesn't mean you're superhuman. Make your own choices, but don't be so stubborn you fall over that edge into real trouble. Cut yourself some slack. You can't protect the world."

"I'm not—" Lack of sleep and unease over Jade had Alex ready to snap at a man who didn't deserve it. He puffed his cheeks and let the breath out slowly. "I know you mean well. I took the transfer to do just that—slow down a little, but then—"

Bob grimaced. "Yeah. Got here just in time to handle a serial killer." He clapped Alex on the shoulder. "You're needed on this one, but I hope you'll give serious consideration to some time off when it's over. Go see your family or hit the beach somewhere—white sand, blue water, half-naked women."

"Sounds like your vacation fantasy, not mine."

"Yeah," Bob chuckled. "Wife won't go along with it,

though, so I'm depending on you to do it and let me live vicariously."

Alex grinned. "Anything for a friend—" His cell phone rang. "Sandoval."

"Alex, we've got a sighting of Rick Howard," Ben Capwell reported.

"Where?"

"He stopped in at Wild Child and asked for his final check. Manager called us."

"Where is he now?"

"Night Dreams."

"You on him?"

"Yeah. Manager stalled long enough for us to get people in place. Patrol unit stayed on him until Sean could take over the tail. Sean's inside. So is Evan."

"Where's our female undercover?"

"She's ready, but I held her back since she's new to the op. If Jade were here—"

But Jade wasn't. And just in case this didn't pan out, he didn't dare pull her from her current assignment. "Lock him down, but do it quietly, as long as there's an option. Make sure everyone understands we can only detain him for questioning right now. Keep it cool. Don't give him a reason to run. I'll be there in fifteen minutes. Good work, Ben. Keep me posted."

He turned to Bob and relayed what he knew. "Have Marco get word to Jade to use her own judgment but call it quits if she manages a good excuse. If necessary, let this op run until the meeting is over, so we don't blow Jade's cover or cause Fleming problems. Then everyone reassemble at the office. I'll give you updates as I have them."

"Done. I hope Howard pans out."

Alex nodded. "Early yet—he might not be our guy. If we

weren't so shorthanded, I'd let the other op run tonight, too, just so we don't lose any time if Howard isn't the one."

"If he is, though, you think about what I said, Alex. Take some time off when this wraps up."

"Yeah, sure." Vacation was the last thing on his mind right now. He raced through a mental checklist while he sprinted to his car.

If she'd had more sleep last night, staying on her game wouldn't be so hard. At the moment, however, Jade wanted very much to tell the guy currently nattering on about Dadaism as it related to New Wave films to get a life. These people were harmless, but so self-absorbed she barely stemmed a scream. And the ones who didn't think they were the real geniuses and everyone else was a hack…that contingent was caught up in a hairsplitting of minutiae boring enough to have her longing to stab her own carotid with the straw in her soft drink.

The cacophony in the lobby rose to the level of pain. She'd had enough. Time to head up to Dan's peaceful aerie and chill out a bit.

She stopped by the rest room first. On the way out, her cell phone rang. She fished it from her purse. "Yes?"

"Abort the…suspect located…" The words crackled and hissed, but the voice sounded like Marco. Cell phones sometimes operated poorly inside big buildings with metal framework.

"Repeat. You're cutting out."

"Movie over…headquarters."

She frowned. "Can you hear me?"

"...yes..."

"Are you saying we're pulling out? To—" she thought back over his words "—return to the office after the movie?"

"Affirmative. Howard...Alex...questioning."

They must have located Rick Howard. "I understand. As soon as possible, I'll head to the office. See you there."

If Howard was their guy, her part in this was over. Lives would be saved, and her disappointment at being finished and returned to the Sex Crimes detail couldn't matter. She'd have to hope that she'd made a strong enough impression to merit consideration for a slot on VICTAF when there was a full-time opening.

She grimaced and stuffed the phone into the special purse with its hidden compartment that held her weapon and badge. She'd pray Doc was impressed, because she'd blown it big-time with Alex. Based on his behavior today, last night's ecstasy came with a monster price tag. Not only would he probably never touch her again, if his aversion to being in the same room with her was any indication, but she'd bet the farm that he'd blackball her from the team.

She was ready to call this night quits so she could go home and hide. Lick her wounds.

And begin the painful process of forgetting not only her career ambitions, but the most amazing night of her life.

She entered the dark hallway behind the concession stand, her spirits dragging. Halfway down, out of the corner of her eye, she saw a shadow flare on the wall—

Just as a cloth enveloped her head—

And a cord squeezed tight around her throat.

Chapter Thirteen

A lex was searching for a place to park in the crowded entertainment district when the radio chatter erupted.

"Something's spooked him," Sean reported. "He acted as though he was going to the bathroom, but he's headed in the wrong direction. Cover the back door. I'm on my way."

Alex swerved into the alley behind the club and slanted his vehicle to block escape. He leaped out and ran toward the club's exit. "Sandoval here—I'm approaching from the east about five hundred yards out. Keep a patrol unit watching the front. Everyone else converge on the alley. Don't let him get free, but I want this guy alive and talking." He drew his weapon and stole through the shadows.

Just then, he heard footsteps pounding. A couple of seconds later, Rick Howard charged in his direction.

Alex stepped from the darkness, weapon clearly displayed. "FBI—stop where you are, Howard."

The blond man slowed, his head swiveling as he looked for an avenue to flee.

"Don't do anything stupid. We only want to ask you some questions."

The man's eyes were frantic, his breath labored. "What for?"

"Where have you been the past three days?"

Howard frowned. "What's it to you?"

"You want to make things tough on yourself, just keep answering a question with a question. You've got answers that check out, we don't have any further business. So I ask you again—how come you disappeared for three days? Why did you quit your job at Wild Child tonight?"

Footsteps neared. Howard's gaze darted around.

Alex could see the temptation on his face. "You can run, but then we'll definitely have to cuff you and haul you in."

For an instant, Howard seemed to relax and accept his fate. Alex started toward him, knowing that the team had them surrounded.

Howard took off.

Alex wheeled and dove, knocking him to the ground and flipping him facedown. When he felt Howard gather himself for one more effort, he grabbed one arm and reached for his cuffs. "Don't even think about it. You don't want easy, then you get hard." Alex launched into the Miranda warning while he fastened the restraints.

He lifted Howard to his feet and patted him down. "Well, well." He removed a plastic bag from Howard's front left pocket, displaying small packets of white powder. "What do we have here?" He dipped a finger into one and touched it to his tongue.

He nodded to a patrolman. "Transport him. We'll continue our discussion after he's booked for possession of narcotics, obstruction of justice and resisting arrest."

The patrolman led Howard away. Alex faced the rest of the group. "Okay. Pack it in and let's see what Mr. Howard has to tell us. Sean, report in to Bob and confirm that we have Howard in custody. I hope we get our answers from him, but we can't afford to assume anything yet. I'll let you know how the interview progresses."

He turned to go.

"Alex?" Sean spoke up. "I'd like to watch the interview, if you don't mind."

Alex nodded. "You're welcome to come."

"Jade probably wants to be in on it, too. She'll be disappointed not to have been here."

Alex grimaced. "I'd say that's a given. When you talk to Bob, tell him to relay an invitation to her to meet us at Central Booking."

He cautioned himself against hoping too much that Howard was their guy. Experience had taught him how often the obvious suspect was not the right one.

His opportunity to pursue whatever had leaped to life between him and Jade would come. He'd make sure of that.

But it wasn't their time yet.

Jade awoke in total darkness, struggling to breathe. Thick fabric smothered her face.

She reached to tear it away, only to find her hands bound behind her back.

Dear God, what—

Caution stilled her, though adrenaline screamed for her to fight her way out. Carefully, she flexed her knees, discovering immediately that her feet were strapped together and tied to the bonds on her wrists.

Then she registered the drone of an engine and realized she was in a moving vehicle. How? Who?

The projection booth. The cloth over her face, the cord—

She battled panic. She'd never been able to bear having her face covered, not even by something so innocuous as her bedsheets.

Calm down. Think. Don't let him know you're awake.
Who was he?

She wiggled her fingers, alarmed at how tight the bindings were. Slowly, she twisted her wrists to explore the possibility of loosening the restraints.

Her left one wasn't bound quite as tightly as her right. Wincing at the scrape of the rope, she bit down on her lip to avoid making noise.

Where was her purse? Her weapon?

"Awake, are you?"

Was that—*Dan?* The voice resembled his, but...off somehow.

Menacing. Cold.

She stilled, listening hard to pinpoint the source. How far away was his seat? How could he see her if he was driving and it was night?

Say something else, she willed him. She was at such a disadvantage that she wouldn't give up her only asset, which was any uncertainty he might have over whether or not she was conscious.

"Don't play games with me," he muttered. "I'll show you who's smart."

Dear God.

It was him. Dan. But why?

Forget why, Jade. Pay attention to your surroundings.

A cargo van, she suspected, noting the vibration beneath her through the unpadded floor. His voice was clear enough that she'd guess him to be five feet away, maybe six. That meant she was at the rear of the van and that he couldn't be sure she was awake without stopping.

She flexed her right calf, and her heart sank. Her ankle holster was gone, too. Luring him to stop had few advantages, given the pitiful inventory of the assets on her side, namely none. No weapons, no communications, securely bound.

Only two remained: she wasn't dead yet, and she still had a functioning brain.

Nothing to write home about, but they beat the alternative.

Would anyone have missed her by now? If not, how long before they knew she was gone? And even then, how would they ever figure out who had her?

Into her worry slipped a calming thought.

Alex. He would figure it out. Meantime, her job was clear. Be alert for opportunities to free herself. Buy time for help to come if she couldn't.

All she had to do was stay alive long enough to assist when they located her.

Her stomach contracted, and she barely stifled a laugh that held no mirth. Three girls had gone missing, and two of them had turned up dead. The third might be the same.

The sour tang of despair rose up the back of her throat, a taste Jade had never completely forgotten.

You're doing fine, Jade…everything's going to work out. Suddenly The Voice rose in her head again, and a measure of calm settled into her.

Alex. A terrified girl wanted to beg him to save her again.

The cop, however, understood that he would try but that she couldn't afford to wait for him. She had to assume it was up to her to save herself this time.

Somehow, though, just the simple memory of him strengthened her resolve.

I'll do what I can, but please…hurry, Alex.

Alex stared through the one-way glass into the interview room. Rick Howard swiped a forehead glistening with sweat while the fingers of his other hand tapped on the table.

Alex glanced up at the clock over the door. Where the hell was Jade? Making a suspect cool his heels could work to a cop's advantage at times, but waiting too long might just as easily provide the suspect with the opportunity to collect himself and grow resistant.

Five more minutes, max. He strode to the hallway door and yanked it open—

Just as Bob was reaching for the knob himself. "Sean tells me Jade's not here yet."

"Yeah. When did you guys cancel the op?"

"Marco relayed the message just after you and I hung up. The rest of us headed in, and he waited around for her until Fleming told him she was already gone."

Alex's heart thudded to a stop. "Fleming? Marco didn't talk directly to Jade?"

"I don't know. Why?"

"Find out if anyone's spoken to Jade since Marco let her know to come in. How long ago was that?"

"Forty-five minutes or so. Marco wasn't too happy that Jade took off without—hey—"

But Alex was already hitting the speed dial on his phone. He wanted to charge forth in a dead run, yet he had no idea where to go.

Fleming. Could it be? Had he sent Jade straight into the arms of a killer?

His instincts had been obscured by the power of his feelings for Jade. Some serial killers got their jollies from being helpful. They liked hanging around the scene of the crime. Some even led the police straight to their victims.

He knew all that but hadn't trusted his reactions to Fleming, concerned that his dislike for the guy had been only jealousy.

When Marco answered, Alex shot straight to the point. "What was Jade's response when you told her the op was canceled?"

"Hard to say. Her reception was bad inside the theater."

"Are you sure she understood the message?"

"Yeah. She filled in the blanks and correctly repeated what she thought I was trying to say."

"Any indication she planned to go somewhere else?"

"She said she'd leave as soon as she could. I'd made a decent contact, so I decided to hang around a little longer and see what else I could learn. I thought Jade should know someone on the team was still there."

"What did Fleming do after he told you Jade had left?"

"Said he had to return to the projection booth. He wasn't real happy that she'd split, but I explained about the op being canceled. He seemed to take it in stride."

"How soon after that did you leave?"

"Immediately."

"Did you see Jade's car in the parking lot?"

"I wasn't looking—Oh, man. Don't tell me—"

Alex cut him off. "Where are you now?"

"At the office."

"Get the closest unit to check the theater, determine if Fleming's still there. Look for Jade's vehicle and get inside the theater to find out if he has her."

Bob's eyes widened.

"Run Fleming's vehicle and put out an APB." He turned back to Marco. "Canvass everyone who was on-site when Jade first arrived. Put together a list of the vehicles you can remember being there at the beginning and which ones remain, in case he didn't drive his own tonight."

"Done. What else?"

What else? Alex forced his mind to go cold. "Alert Tactical to assemble a SWAT team. Compile a roster of the negotiators for APD, DPS and Travis County."

"You gonna take this one yourself?" Marco asked.

Only in my worst nightmare. "We'll see. First we have to ascertain her whereabouts and hope to God she's just grabbing a cup of coffee on her way in."

"But you don't think so."

"No."

"I'll get this under way. Call me with anything else." Marco clicked off.

Bob was on hold while Fleming's car registration was being run. "You suspected him all along."

A greasy fear stained Alex's throat. "I didn't like him, but I didn't trust my gut—" He slammed a fist into the wall. "I knew, goddamn it. I should never have let her go. If I hadn't—"

What? Made love to her? Been trying to fight the urge to protect her?

Bob placed a hand on his arm. "We can't be sure that he has her, Alex. And she's a good cop. She can take care of herself."

"You saw those girls, Bob. What he did to them—" Alex wiped one hand over his face.

"She's not a college kid. She's not vulnerable the way they were."

But she had been. And he'd let her down then, too.

Alex clenched one fist. This wasn't helping.

"Jordan," Bob said into his phone, then frowned. "We may have an officer in trouble, pal. Hurry up." He looked up at Alex. "So you gonna kick this guy Howard?"

Alex glanced toward the interview room. They didn't have any facts yet. He couldn't let a suspect go, simply because his gut was telling him that someone else was their man.

But how he itched to spring into action. He stared at his phone, wishing Marco would call back, saying that Jade had decided to have a whole damn meal on her way to the office. He'd love to discover that there was no reason to worry, that he only needed to read her the riot act—

Just this once, Jade, please be a screwup. Be irresponsible or lazy or have a bad attitude, but—

Be safe. Be alive.

"There's something between you and her, isn't there?" Bob asked.

Alex was set to deny it. He changed his mind. Someone needed to be objective about this. He couldn't. "Yeah. Twelve years' worth." He proceeded to relate the events of that fateful night so long ago. He didn't go so far as to talk about the events of last evening. That, at least for now, was only his and Jade's business.

"Oh, man," Bob responded when he finished. "But you realize that it wasn't your fault, don't you?"

"No one else was negotiating."

"Don't give me that. We've all seen trigger-happy tactical officers."

"It doesn't matter now."

"Bullshit." Bob nodded toward the interview room. "Anyway, let me talk to this fellow."

Alex was about to refuse, when Bob's look turned intent as he listened to his phone. He yanked his notepad out of his shirt pocket and flipped it open. "Repeat that. Gray '92 Corolla, license Tom Baker Charlie seven zero six. Got it. Thanks." He tore off the sheet and handed it to Alex. "I'm taking Howard. You have an op to run. If it turns out to be nothing, we'll switch places."

"Bob—"

"You'd do it for me, buddy. Just keep me up to date. I

hope your famous hunches are dead wrong this time."

"Me, too." Alex grabbed the sheet of paper and flipped open his phone.

The van bumped down a rocky road, jostling Jade, once slamming her into the side and making her cry out as her head smacked into unyielding metal.

"I thought so," called out the voice from the front. "You don't understand who you're dealing with. You can't lie to me."

The throbbing at her temple momentarily distracted her from the tightness in her chest. The cloth on her face had her panting fast and hard.

She couldn't breathe. *Slow down, Jade. There's air...take it easy.*

But she couldn't. The dust in the heavy fabric clogged her nose. Filled her lungs. Oh, God—

Finally, the van braked to a stop. The driver's door opened, then slammed shut.

Jade was ready to whimper. To plead. *Please. Oh, please get it off me—*

The back door opened. A hand grabbed her arm and yanked.

She hit the ground hard. Tried to curl to protect herself—

But she was still bound. She inhaled, prepared to beg.

The cloth was sucked into her mouth, and panic crawled up her chest. A sob escaped. "Please—" With a monstrous effort, she choked off the rest.

"That's more like it."

She thought he might have crouched beside her, but between the blinding ache in her head and her starved lungs, she was losing the ability to think straight.

Save me, Alex, cried out a much younger Jade.

She squeezed her eyes closed. Forced herself to shut down, stop gasping for air. *Focus. Calm. You can breathe through this cloth if you slow down. You're dead if you don't get a grip.*

She forced herself to count: *In, one, two, three. Out, one, two, three.*

Again. In, one, two—

"I thought you were different." This voice was Dan's, except sad.

Out, one, two—

The rope around her throat tightened. "But you aren't, not really. You're just like all the other beautiful ones."

Jade's back arched as she fought for air. "Dan, please—" she choked out.

Suddenly, the cord loosened. Jade sagged in relief.

"Good. I like to hear you beg. Now, let's go inside."

How could she make him leave her out here? Chances were great that the scene of his killings was within the walls of wherever they were. "Dan—"

"What?" He sounded impatient. "There will be time to talk once we're in there." But still he didn't move. "I wasn't prepared for you. The others were smaller, and they wanted what I could offer. You're too tall." Disgust colored his tone. "I can't carry you inside."

An opening. "I'll walk. We're still friends, aren't we, Dan?" *Keep it personal. Don't let him see you as an object. An object's easy to kill.*

"We seemed to be." Wistfulness. "Then you called me sweet. You never meant to honor that rain check, did you? You felt sorry for me." Fury now. "Women use that word *sweet* when they feel superior. I'm a man, not a damn mascot."

"Of course you're not," she soothed. "You're extremely smart and observant." *Oh, please God, uncover my face.*

He laughed then. "I'm smarter than any of you VICTAF hotshots, but does anyone offer me a spot on the team? No."

"I could talk to Alex and Doc. They've seen your work. They know—" She inhaled fibers and dust from the burlap and began to cough. "Dan, please remove this. I can't breathe."

"Once I would have cared about that, Jade. A lot. Back when you made me believe that you really meant to go out with me."

Everything in her screamed for air. She dug down deep for control. "I did mean it," she gasped. Then seized on an idea. "Look into my eyes and see the truth." Another cough wracked her already sore throat. The motion ratcheted up the pain in her head.

"You lie every day in your job. It's all an act."

Despair gripped her. Panic. "Try me." *Hold on, hold on, hold on*, she chanted to herself. *Don't lose it now.*

The silence went on for aeons. She began to wonder if he was still there.

Then, abruptly, a thump in the dirt beside her.

Fingers moved against the cord.

Hurry, hurry, hurry. She bit her lip not to say it aloud.

At last, he yanked the cloth from her face. Jade sucked in great gulps of sweet, blessed air.

For a second.

Then he jerked at the cord.

Still there. Dear God. Around her throat.

"Open your eyes."

Jade forced herself to recall the man she'd first met, so kind and earnest. Then she complied, willing all other thoughts away.

The face that she saw wasn't the one she'd known. She concentrated on the image she needed to portray. She had to find the kind, earnest man inside the stranger before her.

His gaze bored into hers for endless seconds, then he rose unsteadily and cast the hood to the ground. "I can't tell," he muttered. "I don't know what to believe anymore."

She had to reach him. "Then talk to me, Dan. We are friends. I like you, and you like me. Come sit down and explain what's bothering you." She injected only patience and reassurance into her voice, though her strained joints cried out for relief and the cord was tight enough to instill fear.

She couldn't lose her wits; she had to settle him down. She'd just have to endure.

He paced in his halting gait, mumbling to himself. Then he whirled and pointed an accusing finger. "It's you—all of you." One hand raked through his hair. "The pretty ones, the beautiful girls who never see a guy, who make him invisible when he's a man, not a puppy dog, not some kid brother, even if—"

He broke off and stared at her. "You weren't like them, Jade. You didn't pity me. You were going to go out with me."

"I still will," she said. "Dan, I could talk better if you'd let me up. Would you do that, please? Untie me so I could sit here and we could visit—"

His laughter grated on her hearing. "You really think I'm stupid, don't you? Women believe that they can flash their legs and breasts at us, turn us into idiots." He stopped, studying her sadly. "It's too late, don't you get it? I didn't want to kill anyone, but she forced me..." His eyes went unfocused. "I was going to make her famous and show them all. Demonstrate my power. The cripple would blow everyone else out of the water with this film, and finally they'd all shut up about the bastard who was only a sperm donor—"

He clamped his mouth shut. "It doesn't matter. Too late." He sighed deeply, and his shoulders sagged. "The girl tried to run, and I had to stop her." He stared at Jade, bewildered. "Why did she do that? She gave me no choice."

Then he shrugged and withdrew a rectangular object from his pocket.

A knife?

Some of the wounds are premortem. Jade was painfully aware of how vulnerable her position was.

"Now you lie to me. Ask too many questions. You're leaving me no options, Jade, and that makes me really sad."

A snick, and the switchblade glinted, deadly as sharks' teeth.

Chapter Fourteen

Sean met Alex as he strode into the office, his worry echoed on the faces around them. "The whole team is here, Alex. Doc's headed in, along with the rest of VICTAF. Patrol units are calling to see if they can help. What do you need us to do?"

Work. It was the only answer to the urgency seething inside him. Hitting the streets himself, tearing the town apart as he wanted to do so badly, would accomplish nothing.

He was a leader. He'd lead. "Conference room, everyone. Let's put our heads together."

The team required only seconds to assemble. "Start telling me everything you know about Dan Fleming, people. You first, Sean. Property—where does he live? Own or rent?"

"Owns a small house off Fifty-first near Duval. Been there four years."

"Warrant to search the premises?"

Case Maxwell spoke up. "Paperwork's under way. I got an unhappy judge out of bed, but she listened to my case and I think she's on board. She wants to see the affidavit. It's being delivered right now."

"That's not good enough," he snapped.

"We have to have probable cause, Alex. A hunch doesn't cut it. The guy has no record of criminal activities, not even a parking ticket."

Alex rapped his knuckles on the table. "Yeah. I know." *But it's him, damn it.* Suddenly, he frowned. "Where's Evan?"

"Here," Evan said from the doorway. "I was at DPS, checking internal records."

Doc walked up behind Evan. "On Fleming?"

"Yeah. Twenty-six years old, born in Iowa, father unknown, mother died last year in Austin."

"Job history?"

"Didn't graduate from UT film school. A year and a half with a photo lab, followed by his current position at DPS."

"When did his mother move to Austin?"

"Same year he started at DPS. Took a steady job to be able to support her is my guess."

"I imagine you're right. So why does he stay?"

"State jobs are usually secure."

"But they don't pay well."

"There's something more important." Evan's eyes met Alex's. "It's not good."

"Spill it." The itch between Alex's shoulder blades got worse.

"He's not Dan Fleming."

"What?" A hubbub filled the room.

"I went after fingerprints while I was waiting for the full personnel file on him." He waited a beat. "He doesn't have any."

The dull roar inside Alex's head ratcheted upward. "Aren't all employees' fingerprints on file?"

"Yeah."

"So, what—he deleted them? How did he get access?"

"He shouldn't be able to. But here's the zinger—Dan Fleming didn't exist until four years ago. His social security number belongs to a dead guy."

Alex glanced at Doc. Doc nodded. "I'll call D.C., but if he's clean…"

"I understand." Fear for Jade was a snake coiled in Alex's gut. "Case, this should help your judge make up her mind."

"Maybe. This is Travis County, remember. The law-and-order crowd isn't popular here." His expression hardened. "I'll get it for you somehow." He pulled his phone from his pocket and left the room.

Alex turned to the faces looking at him from around the table. "All right, people, let's tear this guy's life apart. Unravel his disguise from the point where he started it. Ben and Sean, you work on his credit report and track back to his applications. Analyze his expenses. Marco, you tackle phone records. Charlie, access the deed records and search for other property in his name. Tap adjoining counties, too." He glanced around. "He's got her—I'm sure of it. She's smart and strong, but he's a killer and someone she thought she could trust. He probably took her unaware." He clenched his jaw so hard he thought his teeth might crack. "We are not finding Jade in a warehouse, folks. That's not going to happen."

Expressions grim, they all rushed out to tackle the assigned jobs.

Leaving Alex to stare at the scarred tabletop and bend the pencil in his hand until it snapped.

Dan's eyes went flat and cold as moonlight flashed over the blade.

Jade held his gaze, some instinct telling her that whatever of the friendly man was left inside couldn't kill her in cold blood. She had to keep him calm and maintain some connection.

If she glanced away, she became prey.

With a twist of the wrist, he arced the blade through the air and paused to admire it. "This was his." The smile chilled her.

She was almost afraid to speak, but more so not to keep him engaged. "Whose?"

The smile vanished. The pupils narrowed. "The bastard who made me and walked away."

I'm sorry, she started to say, then remembered how he hated pity. "It was his loss."

Dan showed surprise and cocked his head, considering. Then he grinned like a delighted child. "It was, wasn't it?" His face cleared, and the man she'd known earlier reappeared. He went to his knees beside her. With one quick slice, he severed the rope connecting her wrists and ankles.

"Oh—" Jade collapsed suddenly. Her strained joints screamed. "Thank you." She weighed her options, and decided to take a risk. "Dan, I—" She broke off and ducked her head. "This is embarrassing, but I need—" She cleared her throat. "To, uh, go…" She held her breath, waiting to see if her gambit would work.

Looking at him was confusing, and she wished for better light. Something vulpine and deadly stalked over the kind features of the man she'd met, the two tangling in an unholy dance.

But the predator slipped back beneath his skin. The other man blushed. "Oh. Yeah—okay." He sliced the cords from her ankles, but backed away quickly.

Damn. If her muscles weren't cramping so badly, she would have struck out at him with her legs, but with her arms locked behind her back, she feared for her balance.

"Thank you." Without grace, she rose. "Would you—"

She turned and held out her wrists.

"Oh—sure." He stepped forward. Then halted, just out of reach.

She'd only get one chance, she thought. With ruthless restraint, she remained still.

He laughed, and the sound of it wasn't pretty.

The predator was back. "What kind of idiot do you think I am?" He approached, tossing the knife as if he hadn't a care in the world. His smile was wide and eerily like the ones he'd brandished as her friend.

But his eyes...

"I meant no insult, Dan." With effort she kept her tone reasonable. Calm, though fear ran roughshod inside her. "It's only that—" She shrugged and hit the note of apology again. "My hands. Women have to—you know—" She blinked rapidly, and the moisture that gathered wasn't all faked. She made her voice nearly a whisper. "My pants, I can't—"

Two men jockeyed for position in his expression then. She wasn't sure she'd ever seen anything more chilling.

And her life lay in the balance.

The wrong man won. He looped the end of the noose around his arm several times, inexorably drawing her forward. "You never cared when you were humiliating me before. Why should I give a rat's ass for your discomfort?"

Jade couldn't argue; she could barely breathe. *You're not choking*, she lectured herself. *The rope is tight, but you can get air.*

Images of another night, another captor, flickered like a runaway projector. *Pick up the phone. I said pick it up—*

An involuntary whimper escaped her.

His eyes narrowed. "You're scared." A smile spread. "Excellent. You should respect me."

The pretty ones, the beautiful girls who never see a guy, who make him invisible.

She had to clear her mind of the past and focus on handling this man while she remained alert for signs of the sane Dan with whom she had a bond, however tenuous.

Power. The predator wanted power. If she could placate him, maybe she could stay alive long enough for Alex to find her.

"I respect you." She bowed her head as if saluting.

"Is that right?" Pleasure smoothed out his tone. "That's good, that's very good."

Then cunning overlaid it. "Inside," he commanded. "You want help? I know just the person."

Alex paced the bullpen and rained down silent curses on his head for not saving some angle of investigation for himself. This dead time while he waited for answers from others was what he hated about supervising. Usually, he had other cases to work on, but at the moment, his concentration was shot to hell. Nothing else mattered until Jade was found.

Safe. Please let her be alive. Please.

He stalked to the coffeepot and stared at it, wondering how much more his stomach lining could handle. He wanted so badly to tear the town apart, conduct a house-to-house search for her—

Barely, only barely, he resisted the urge to smash his fist into the nearest wall.

What was he missing? Damn it, there had to be some angle on Fleming he'd overlooked.

He spun on his heels and made his way to her desk.

And stopped dead, gripping the back of her chair.

He could smell her, the faintest scent of her.

Oh, Christ.

All the images he'd been staving off flooded him then. Jade, so generously sharing the heaven of her body. Beneath him, the wild luxury of her hair streaming over his sheets…above him, a carmine curtain sealing out the world. Her fingers tracing his grandmother's portrait…her hesitance to intrude on his sanctuary.

How her hips felt in his hands, her skin so soft over supple muscle and stunning curves—

And her eyes, mossy green and so expressive.

Hurt, the last time he'd seen them.

And all his fault, because he didn't know how to handle the teeming, messy welter of emotions she stirred inside him.

His gaze seized on a note on her calendar.

"Her dog," he murmured.

From the adjoining desk, Sean raised his head. "What?"

"Jade's dog. Where does he stay? Inside or outside?"

Sean lifted his shoulders. "I don't know."

"Anyone met her neighbors?"

Around the room, heads shook.

It made no sense, but he wanted to do this one thing for her as a sign of faith that she'd return to that dog who was her sole companion. A propitiation to higher forces, maybe. He wheeled back to the desk, and suddenly, something struck him—

Companion. "The mother." He said it louder. "Fleming's mother. He bought the house, took the job at DPS because his mother was ill and needed a place to live."

Excitement surged through the room like volts of electricity.

"Marco," Alex called out. "Send a unit to Jade's place to check on her dog. Make sure he's not stuck inside."

"Will do."

"Okay. Let's assume the mother isn't fictional. Evan, check his insurance at DPS for claims for a dependent. Obtain the name for us. If she's real, unless he's been planning this for a very long time, enough to give her a false identity, too, we just might get lucky and track him through her.

"If she's listed, give Charlie the name to add to his search of deed records. Sean, run that name through the credit bureau."

Case walked back inside and flipped his phone shut. "Warrant is ready."

Yes. "Still no activity at his home, Marco?"

The sergeant shook his head. "All quiet."

"I'll meet the technicians there." Alex charged for the door, pausing to speak over his shoulder to Doc. "Call me the second anything turns up."

"You bet."

Alex quickened his pace. *Hang on, Jade. I'll find you, I swear I will.*

No other outcome could be considered.

Waves slapping the shore, that was it. As Dan led her like a dog on a leash into a darkened room, Jade finally recognized the faint sound she'd been hearing.

They were on one of the lakes—but which one? The manmade chain of six Highland Lakes formed from the Colorado River extended eighty-five miles north and west of Austin. Furiously, she tried to gain any sense of how long they'd traveled. The way roads meandered in the Hill Country, they could be as close as Lake Austin or perhaps on the shores of Lake Travis. But Travis itself was sixty miles long.

That meant a lot of shoreline to explore.

Her eyes began to adjust to the darkness; she searched for a phone and the locations of exit doors and windows.

Nothing luxurious here, only a simple lake cabin. In the moonlight shining through a sliding glass door, she spied a threadbare plaid sofa and an old recliner. Beyond the sofa, she saw that this house was built on a cliff; the water lay far below. She squinted, scanning for landmarks, but found nothing familiar. All the lakes had portions with cliff frontage, to her knowledge.

"Come on—" He yanked the cord and shoved her past a room where she thought she glimpsed a tripod.

She slowed to get a better look.

"You said it was urgent." He reached for a doorknob and twisted, revealing stairs descending into a gaping black maw.

Instinctively, she resisted going down into who-knew-what horrors. "Hold on—"

"I don't want to." His tone was plaintive. "I'm tired of wishing for my turn. I prayed for the bastard to come back and claim me. She promised he'd give us the money for the operation that would fix my leg. He never did either one. Then I had to stick around for that whiny bitch to die and set me free—" He whirled on her, reeling her close. "I waited for you, too, Jade. You were like Carly, only better. She was nice, not vain as the other two were. Not that pretty, so it wasn't the same for her to respect me, but—"

He shrugged. "Then there you were, beautiful and strong, but you treated me fine. I knew you'd understand that I never meant to hurt that girl, and you'd help me explain it." He tightened his grip to the point of pain while his face screwed up and his eyes howled misery. "None of this was supposed to happen. I only wanted to make a film that would force people to recognize that they should never have looked past me, never made fun of me or patted me on the head and—"

He averted his face, but not before she saw tears spring to his eyes.

"Dan, it's not too late. We can work this out. I know you'd never hurt anyone. Let me call Alex and tell him—"

"No—" He shook his head violently. "I have to think. Shut up and let me think—"

"I can help you. Let's sit down and talk, Dan—"

"Shut up, shut up, shut up!" He dropped the coils and slapped at her, shoving her away—

The push unbalanced her—

And sent her tumbling into the dark hole.

Chapter Fifteen

A drenaline fired through Alex's system as he stepped into the small house. He paused just inside the living room and glanced around while he slipped on the thin gloves.

His first impression was of a typical bachelor pad: comfortable furniture without an appreciable decorating scheme. No housekeeper, for sure. Newspapers and magazines were strewn over the coffee table. A couple of beer cans stood sentinel amid them.

High-end television and sound system. Game player with controller abandoned on the couch.

"Okay," he said to the techs waiting behind him. "Go ahead with this room. I want fingerprints, any mail, DNA samples, of course—"

Computer. There had to be a computer room, maybe shared with Fleming's video equipment. "Canisters of film, photographs, CDs, DVDs, zip drives…go through all of it."

Bypassing the kitchen for now, Alex headed down the short hallway. Single bathroom to the right, towels on the floor, razor on sink, toothpaste tube with cap off.

Not a neat kind of guy, but then, few bachelors were.

Across the hall, a tiny bedroom that would most commonly be the spare showed distinct signs of habitation. Alex pushed the door open farther. Bed unmade, man's clothes strung around. Alarm clock.

Alex frowned. Why wouldn't he take the bigger bedroom for himself?

Then his face cleared. Because Fleming didn't have female company much, if at all. This room was solely for sleeping.

If film was his life, Fleming would take the larger room for that. "Bathroom and first bedroom on the left ready for you," he called as he reentered the hall.

Past this one on the left lay another, smaller room, piled high with film cans and little else. Would tapes of the dead girls be here?

Jade couldn't wait while he looked.

He turned to the tech just coming behind him. "See if anything's recent and examine it. If not, transport all these boxes."

"Sure thing."

One room remained, the door to it firmly shut. Alex leaned nearer.

Closed…and locked.

He wasn't waiting for a ram or a locksmith. Somewhere, Jade was in trouble. He was sure of it.

He reared back and delivered a powerful kick, then a second. The door flew open.

Bingo. No telling how many thousands of dollars Fleming had invested in the cameras and lights and tripods, the computer on the desk…every bit of it clean and carefully positioned. "Here's the computer," he said over his shoulder. "I want everything you can dig out, and I need it yesterday."

"I'm on it."

Alex itched to do the search himself, but though his computer skills were decent, he wasn't prepared to risk losing one iota of data that might lead them to Jade. He examined the room, studying the framed movie posters on the walls for clues to Fleming's taste. Most of them were films he'd never heard of, and the style was at least a couple of decades old.

Then it hit him. He glanced at each one again.

They all had the same director.

He whipped out his phone and hit speed dial. "Doc—tell Charlie to stop what he's doing and search for property under the name of Fleming Daniels. I'll hold."

He stared at the poster in front of him, jiggling the change in his pocket. "Come on, come on," he muttered.

Charlie's voice broke the silence. "A cabin on Lake Travis, near Volente. Bought two years ago."

Right around the time his mother died. *Left you some money, did she?* "Good work, Charlie. I'll contact you if my GPS doesn't give enough detail. Meanwhile, check out the aerial views and get back to me with some idea of what's around this place. And let me talk to Doc."

"Will do."

"Thanks."

Doc picked up. "Evan got a hit on a van registered in that name. Marco remembers seeing it parked near the alley behind the theater."

"I'm on my way."

"I'll call APD SWAT."

Alex's heart sped up. "Keep them on standby only until I reach the scene and assess. We aren't sure that she's there."

"Want Charlie to see if there's a deputy in the area?"

"No. Nothing on the scanner. I don't want news helicopters circling."

"Agreed." Doc paused. "Alex, Bob talked to me."

Alex understood the hidden message. Doc had been told about his past with Jade.

"You want me to take this one?" Doc asked.

"I can handle it, Doc."

"You can't rewrite history."

"I'm not trying to."

Sliding into his car, he expected Doc to tell him that he should stay behind because he was too involved.

And Doc didn't know the half of it.

"All right. I trust you."

Alex understood it was a leap of faith. "She's coming out of there alive. I'll take myself off the case before I'll risk any other outcome."

"I'll be on the scene ASAP." Doc's voice grew quiet. "I got her into this."

A reminder that Alex wasn't the only one who felt responsible for Jade's fate. "I didn't act on my gut feeling about Fleming, Doc. There's plenty of blame to spread around."

Doc merely grunted. "Contact me when you're onsite."

"Yeah." Alex flipped the phone shut and concentrated on his driving.

"Wake up. Please wake up. Please," a faint chant buzzed at Jade's ear.

"Wha—" She raised her head sharply and starbursts exploded behind her eyes. "Unnnh—hurts."

"Be quiet. He'll hear you."

Jade's eyes sprang open. She wasn't imagining things. Who—?

Faint traces of moonlight filtered in through a tiny slit well above her reach. A face appeared above her, barely visible in the gloom. "I'd hoped he was gone for good." The girl paused, and they heard the crashes and bangs above. "He's angry again, just like before. He'll kill you, too. But me first."

Her head swiveled from side to side, her tear-streaked, filthy face pinched with terror. "Me first."

The third girl. Could it be? Jade tried to rise, but the movement pounded hot spikes through her head. She gave up and rolled to her side, panting to keep her gorge down. When she thought she dared, she spoke again. "Are you Carly Woods?"

The girl froze. "How do you know my name?"

"I'm a cop. We've been looking for you."

The girl noted Jade's bound hands, and despair raced over her features. "But you're a prisoner now." In her voice was the thin edge of hysteria.

Jade shoved herself to sitting, despite the nausea. "We probably don't have much time before he comes back. Describe this place to me while you untie my wrists."

"I can't. Untie you, I mean." Fresh tears rolled down her cheeks. "My—my fingers—" She held out her own hands, bound in front of her rather than behind.

Jade leaned closer and barely kept from moaning at the motion. Then she understood. The girl's fingers were fat as sausages because her wrists had been bound so long. "Okay. Calm down. Panic won't help us." Jade's mind raced. "Watch the stairs while you tell me everything you've seen. What's on the ground floor? Is there a phone? Does he have guns?"

"I'm not sure. I was blindfolded until I was locked down here." Her face crumpled. "Tanya told me a girl before her tried to escape and he killed her. Now Tanya's gone."

Jade rolled to her back, gritting her teeth as each bruised muscle touched concrete. "Don't think about them now. Explain what you do know."

"Like what?"

"Start with the physical setup. Does any daylight get in here?"

"Barely." The girl's voice quivered. "And there are spiders and—" She took in a deep breath. "Rats, I think. One of them tried to bite me, but Tanya kicked at it and—" her voice faltered, then firmed "—scared it away."

"I always thought Miss Muffett should have stomped the bejesus out of that spider."

Carly's giggle broke on a sob.

"We're going to make it out. There are others behind me. They'll be here soon." *Please, Alex.*

"Really?" The girl's voice held a fragile note of hope.

"The more facts I have, the more we can help them. Tell me what else is down here besides varmints."

While Carly stumbled over a description, Jade continued to wiggle her arms open wider, attempting to ease her hips through the circle. At the moment, she would have sold her soul for a pair of boyish hips that could slip through with no trouble. Thank heavens he hadn't used zip ties, at least.

She focused on Carly's words and blocked out the ropes cutting into her skin as she forced her hands farther apart.

Carly ended her depressing inventory. "I'm sorry. I tried to find something to use as a weapon before the next time he—" She choked, and Jade could hear the tears again.

"You've been very brave, Carly." And she had. The average coed was completely unprepared to encounter anything like this.

"But he—"

"Hold on. I've almost got it." With a last mighty squeeze, Jade ignored the natural instinct to avoid pain as the ropes tore her flesh. She shoved her hands apart one degree further—

And suddenly, her wrists were behind her thighs. She folded her knees and pushed past the agony in her shoulders—

Free. Hallelujah. Her abraded wrists hurt like hell, her head was primed to explode and she had no interest in seeing the bruises all over her body, but they were a step closer to freedom.

"Let me have your hands." Jade's fingers had little room to maneuver with her wrists still bound, and they'd begun to swell, too, so she was clumsy. Since Dan could reappear at any moment, she put her teeth to use, as well, and nerves didn't help her dexterity.

"I'm sorry," Carly said.

"For what?" Jade didn't look up. Picking at Carly's bonds required every ounce of her focus.

"I—I smell bad. He leaves me here for so long and I'm not sure how many days it's been and—"

At last. Jade lifted her head in triumph, then saw the girl's devastation. She thought Carly could use a hug, but even if Jade could give one at the moment, there was no time for a breakdown.

So she grinned. "Hey, I work with guys all day. I didn't smell a thing."

"How can you joke about this?"

Jade met her gaze squarely. "If we don't keep our heads, we won't get out of here alive." She gentled her voice. "He's sick, Carly, and he's dangerous, but he's not superhuman. We have two advantages. One, we're both smart and strong, and two, help will arrive. When this is over, we can both cry our eyes out, but right now, we have to lock our emotions away and concentrate on staying alive until they overpower him."

"Help is really coming?"

"Absolutely." Jade put every ounce of conviction she could muster into her voice. She craved to believe it herself. "But what would be even better is if we figured out a way to have him out of commission before they get here."

The Good Lord helps those who help themselves, her grandmother always said.

"You think we can?"

The final coil slid off Carly's wrists, and Jade exulted. "You bet I do. Now, I know your fingers hurt, but I need you to untie me. Will you try?"

Carly's smile was tremulous, but her eyes had calmed. "I'll manage."

"Attagirl." Jade chewed at her cheek as she fought the urge to rush Carly. Instead, she decided that Carly could use a future to think of. "So…what's the first thing you want to do after we get out of here?"

The girl's head jerked upward, her eyes sparking with hope. Then she bent to her task again.

"A bath. Definitely a bath."

Jade managed a chuckle. "Yeah, me, too." *Hurry, hurry, hurry.*

She scanned the space around them for possible weapons. When Carly's fingers slipped again, Jade thought a distraction might help. She was about to ask what the second thing was—

When she realized that the din from upstairs had stopped.

Then the door at the top of the steps opened.

The closer he got, the more certain Alex was that this was the place. Secluded, neighbors far away and separated by thick tree cover, Fleming would have all the privacy and time in the world.

Alex watched the GPS and parked well back from the road leading to the cabin. Sounds traveled far at night, especially over water, and the road to the cabin was noisy caliche.

He rose from the car and closed the door carefully, wishing the moon weren't quite so bright. He pulled out his phone and called Doc. "It's very isolated out here. If we have to bring in tactical, have them set up a half-mile back. There's an abandoned house that should work. I'm going to look around."

"I'll be there in twenty. Wait for me."

"I'm won't do anything stupid." *But I have to know if she's there.* "I'm just going to check out the situation." *Before it turns into a circus.*

"Alex—"

"What?"

"Nothing. Report in ten minutes, or I'm on your tail." Doc hesitated. "One more thing. APD's not big on waiting when it's one of theirs. I can't hold them off forever."

But she's mine in the deepest, most personal sense. "Understood."

He shucked off his shirt and replaced it with a black T-shirt he kept in the car with his FBI raid jacket.

Weapon drawn, he set out through the trees.

A footstep scuffed on a stair near the top. They didn't have much time.

Jade leaned next to Carly's ear. "Move into the deepest shadows under the stairs. When I manage to distract him, you run outside as fast as you can. Don't stop until you find help."

"But I can't leave you—"

Jade shook her head violently. "I'm trained in self-defense. He's not much bigger, and I'm more fit. Now, loop the rope back around my wrists but don't tie it."

More footfalls, then the beam of a flashlight sweeping the opposite wall.

"Hurry—and remember what I said. When you get help, ask for Alex Sandoval and advise him that Jade's with Dan Fleming. Tell him I said *pardon me*. He'll understand what that means." *I hope.*

Carly's fingers fumbled as she wound the cord around Jade's wrists. "I'm scared."

"Of course you are, but you're not going to let me down."

The girl nodded vigorously.

"Now, get over there and don't make a sound. Watch for your chance. Don't dare stop or we're both dead."

Jade swiftly made her way to the corner that would take Dan farthest from Carly. She eased to the floor and lowered her lids, watching for him behind the screen of her lashes.

Light swept the concrete, and she shut her lids completely, every other sense alert for his passage.

"Jade? Where are you? I'm sorry—I didn't mean to harm you. You're not injured, are you?" His voice sounded weak and uncertain.

Please, Carly, don't be misled.

"Oh, no." He dropped to his knees in front of her as she lay on her side, forcing her breathing to remain even and slow despite the racing of her heart. "What's wrong? It's not supposed to happen this way." He grabbed her shoulder and shook. "You can't be hurt—"

The plaintive tone fractured. "Jade, wake up." A rougher shaking now, his voice harsher. "Don't you dare do this to me. It's not fair."

His touch vanished. "Carly? Where are you?"

Jade heard him start to rise and groaned to draw his attention. *Run, Carly. Now.*

She fluttered her lids. "Wha—what happened?" She

opened her eyes. "Dan?" She sensed movement behind him.

So did he.

She tried to rise. "I'm hurt, Dan. Are you all right? Where are we?" She looked down, then up quickly. "Why are my arms tied—"

He grabbed her throat. "Where is she?"

"Who?" From the corner of one eye, she thought she saw Carly pause at the bottom of the stairs.

She didn't dare check. Instead, she locked her gaze on his. "Dan, I don't understand—"

At the sound of Carly's footsteps, he whirled, still on his knees.

"Come back here," he shouted, and rose.

Carly faltered and looked back.

"Run, Carly! Run!" Jade struggled with the cord on her wrists.

Dan howled an inhuman sound and charged.

She couldn't let him get Carly. Wrists still tangled in the cord, Jade shoved to her feet and dove at his back.

The flashlight flew from his hand as they both went down. Jade's head hit the bottom step hard enough to rattle her teeth.

He scrambled up again. "Stop—" he yelled after Carly, and grabbed the rail.

Jade blinked rapidly to clear her vision and gathered herself for another effort.

The door above them slammed.

Dan roared his rage.

Then turned on her, his face a mask of fury—

The stiletto once more gleaming in his hand.

Chapter Sixteen

At the corner of the cabin, Alex stopped.

What was that sound?

He scanned the area while he listened.

There. Voices, but muffled. They should be clearer, as close as he was to the house. Could the house have a basement? In these limestone hills, that wasn't likely but not impossible. If not a basement, an interior room?

He was going in. He pulled out his phone to alert Doc—

The front door burst open, and a figure charged through at a dead run, sobbing and wheezing.

"Halt—" He leveled his weapon. "FBI. Stop where you are. Move out from that shadow."

The slender figure staggered toward him. "Are you—she told me to get help—"

"Who? Jade?"

"He has her. She told me to get help—" Hysteria bubbled up from her throat. "Alex. She told me to find Alex."

He lowered his weapon and approached. "That's me. Are you Carly Woods?"

She swiped at her nose and sobbed. "Yes. He's going to kill her. He's murdered the others and he's going to—"

"Hold on. Where inside?"

"D-downstairs."

"Does he have any weapons?"

"I don't know."

"Is Jade hurt?"

She nodded. "He shoved her down the stairs earlier, and just now she jumped him to give me time—"

"Do the stairs creak?"

"No. They—they're concrete." She looked devastated. "I wanted to stay and help, but—"

"You did fine." He hit Doc's number on speed dial. "Doc, I'm going inside. Jade and Fleming are in the basement. Carly Woods is safe, and she'll be watching for you at the road with details."

"Can you wait for us?"

"No. She's hurt and fighting with him now. He barricades them inside, and he holds all the cards. Tactical could never break in without loss of life. I'm not having her go through that again."

"So you're going to negotiate with him?"

"I'll do whatever it takes to get her out alive. Bring paramedics and keep Tactical under control. I'll try to keep my cell open so you can tell what's going on."

"Alex—" Doc sighed.

"This can't wait, Doc. This guy is decompensating fast. I won't be stupid, but Jade's out of time. I gotta go."

He shoved the phone in his pants pocket without disconnecting.

"Any lights down there?" he asked the girl. "Windows?"

"Only a tiny one. He had a flashlight, but he lost it when Jade jumped him."

"Where were they when you last saw them?"

"It sounded like someone hit the stairs. Please...save her."

You saved me, she'd said about the past. But he hadn't.

"Alex."

He glanced back, impatient to be gone.

"She said—" The girl shook her head. "She told me to say *pardon me* to you, that you'd know what that meant. Do you?"

Echoes of that night so long ago. *Say pardon me if he's standing right beside you*, he'd asked her.

Jade was trapped with a killer again yet making plans for her own rescue. What a woman. "Yeah. Thanks. Watch for Doc."

He buried his dread and moved as silently as possible.

Praying he'd make it in time.

The knife slashed down in a deadly arc. "On your knees, bitch."

"Dan—"

"On your knees!" he screamed. "Don't you see what you've done? You've ruined everything." With his free hand, he tore at his hair, his movement in the reflected beam of the fallen flashlight casting a monstrous shape onto the concrete wall.

Fury contorted his features into a mask that wasn't human.

"I'm sorry, Dan. I never meant to." Behind her back, Jade frantically worked at tangled rope Carly had rewrapped around her wrists.

At last—one hand was free, then the other. She needed to stall him. "Nothing has to be ruined. It wasn't your fault." *Hurry, Carly.* "You were a victim."

His head rose. "Don't patronize me. I'm sick of being considered harmless. Neutered." His blond hair shifted over his cheek. "I'm a man. I only wanted someone to see the real me." He glared at her. "I thought you did, but it was all a lie, wasn't it?"

Jade ignored the fact that he was a killer and concentrated on the rapport they'd had. "I honestly like you. You're smart and attractive."

"You don't mean that." The nice guy slid away, and the predator approached. "I've seen you and Sandoval." Dan nearly spat out the name while his eyes went flat and reptilian. "You think I don't notice how he looks at you? He couldn't stand it that you were going out with me."

His head swung around, then back, his eyes accusing. "I bet the two of you had a good time, laughing about the lame-o from the lab who'd asked you for a date."

"No, Dan. You're wrong." Jade inched her legs beneath her, readying for defense as his agitation increased. "We never did that."

"Liar—" Lightning-fast, he swooped down and grabbed a fistful of her hair. "Bitch—" He revolved his wrist one time, wrapping the hair tightly, and yanked hard.

Jade tried to ignore the pain in her scalp; uncoiling one leg, she lashed out at his bad leg.

He yelled and fell to the floor. The knife tumbled from his grip, but he didn't release her.

Her head hit the concrete, and she fought back the sickening dizziness, scrabbling across the rough floor—

Dan jerked hard on her hair and leaned down.

Coming up, victorious, brandishing the blade. "You think you're so superior, but I'll show you." He slashed at her, and vicious pain erupted in her arm.

She attempted to twist away, but a tearing sensation in her scalp stopped her cold.

"Beg me. Tell me who's better now."

A voice spoke from the stairs. "Dan. It's Alex Sandoval. I'm here to help you. Tell me what you want."

Alex. *There's nothing to say until I see that goddamn van out front.* Kirk's words echoed in her ears, and all of a sudden, she was fifteen again.

"Get out of here or she's dead," Dan screamed. "Drop your weapon, or I'll kill her. I swear it." With surprising quickness, he caught her neck in the crook of his arm, then pushed the blade into her throat. She stifled a cry.

"Your flashlight is on the floor over here, Dan." Alex's voice was slow and soothing. "I just want to help you see where you're going."

"I'm not moving. Get out of here." Dan's breathing was rapid.

"Sure," Alex said. "But I bet you're tired and thirsty. Why don't you let me help you?"

"I don't need anyone's assistance. I'm not a cripple."

"Of course you're not," Alex consoled.

Had he moved slightly closer? After one involuntary flinch, Jade forced herself to remain still, but the blade pricked her skin. Blood started trickling down her neck.

"Stop right there. I'm not kidding. I'll kill her."

The ray from Dan's flashlight bisected the floor near where she thought Alex was standing. He would have to cross it to approach them, compromising his night vision. Dan would see him before Alex could focus on them.

Alex was only too aware of the problem. "Let Jade talk to me," he said.

"You don't call the shots—" Fleming's voice rose.

"I can help you, Dan. I'd like to make this go away." *For Jade, that is.* He wanted to snap Fleming's neck with his bare hands. Ruthlessly, he clamped a lid on the violence boiling inside him. "First step is for me to hear Jade tell me she's unharmed."

"You can't fix this," Fleming said.

Jade's soft gasp of pain was a claw raking Alex's insides.

Echoes of the past reverberated down his spine. *Not now.* With effort, Alex narrowed his focus to the moment. "You didn't mean any of this to happen, did you, Dan?"

"No." Fleming's voice wavered slightly.

Pinpointing the direction, Alex sidestepped to avoid entering the beam. "I believe you. Now, let Jade talk to me."

A long, deadly silence ensued.

Alex waited what felt to be hours. He opened his mouth to try another tack—

"Pardon me, Dan," Jade said, her tone nearly calm. "But it's Alex's right to know that I've only got two cuts."

"Shut up. He has no rights here."

Alex thought rapidly, processing her comments. *Good for you, Jade.* Fleming was next to her, to Alex's right, and he had a knife.

"How badly is she bleeding? If she loses too much blood, she might go limp and fall." Alex edged another few steps toward them, pleading silently for her to remember other instructions from that long-ago night. *Don't fight him. Go limp and fall.*

"I didn't want to hurt her, but she forced me." Fleming's voice vibrated. "None of this was supposed to happen."

Alex zeroed in on their location, just around a stack of old furniture, as he withdrew a small but powerful penlight from his pocket. He was too close to risk speaking again.

He edged nearer, praying that Jade had understood his message and would drop to give him a clear shot.

Just then, footsteps shuffled over loose rocks outside.

"What is that?" Fleming screamed.

Damn it, damn it—Alex leaped and flicked the switch—

Catching sight of Fleming with one arm around Jade's chest, trapping her upright.

In his hand, he gripped a stiletto, sleek and lethal, pressing it into her throat just over her carotid artery. "Call them off." Fleming shouted. "And drop your gun, or I'll kill her right now."

"I can't call them off until Jade's free. I wish I could, Dan, truly." Alex held his weapon steady, his pulse roaring in his ears.

Their heads were so close. Too close.

"You're lying. You're in charge. You can tell them to leave."

"I want to, Dan. Let her go, and I will."

"No." Fleming's head shook frantically. "No, that won't work." He pressed the blade harder, and Jade gasped. "Get that light out of my eyes."

"Lower the knife, and I will."

"Get it out of my eyes!" Fleming jerked the knife upward—

Too late, too late—Alex narrowed his focus to a tiny spot on Fleming's forehead.

The blade plunged downward, swift and deadly—

Alex squeezed the trigger—

Fleming's momentum folded him over Jade.

She cried out—

And collapsed beneath Fleming's weight.

Everything in Alex died in that instant.

With a roar, he charged across the dirt toward her. *No. No*—

He shoved Fleming aside, barely pausing to see the ruined skull as he fell on his knees before Jade. Within him howled a pain so enormous that all other sounds vanished into a vacuum.

She stirred then, and attempted to push upward. "Alex—"

Heart thundering, Alex grabbed her with unsteady hands and folded her into his arms. "Did he get you? Let me look."

He couldn't see the knife. He felt around for it with one hand.

"Are you okay?" Jade gasped.

He was shaking so hard he wasn't sure he could speak. "Fine."

"Dan—is he—?"

"Dead." Rage swept over him then. "I wish I could kill him again." Damn it, he needed more light. He leaned her back gently.

Her fingers tightened. "Don't let me go, not yet. I can't seem to quit trembling."

"I won't, but I have to see, baby."

The knife clattered to the floor.

Thank heaven. It wasn't buried in her. Just to be sure, he slid one hand down her side—

And encountered something slick and warm and wet.

Oh, God.

Above them, he heard footsteps and sirens.

"Down here—" he shouted. "Medic—now!"

"How did they know?"

"My cell is on in my pocket." *Hurry, hurry.*

A dark stain was spreading over her entire left side.

"You have a habit of saving me." Her attempted cheer ended on a wobble.

"I didn't—I should have—"

"Stop that. I don't want to hear it." She placed her fingers over his lips. "It's only a cut on my arm…" Her glance followed his. "Oh." Her breath turned shallow, her voice faint and bemused. "My side. I'm…bleeding."

"Hold on, honey. Help is here. You're going to be fine." *Don't take her from me*, he pleaded with whatever force was listening. *Not now. Please. I haven't told her—*

Her eyes hazed over.

"Jade, stay with me—" He tried to stem the bleeding with his free hand.

Like a child's rag doll, she sagged in his arms.

Blinded by fear, Alex lifted her and turned to see Doc at the bottom of the stairs, his eyes dark with concern.

"Damn it, where are they?" Alex's fingers tightened on her. "She's not going to die. I won't let her."

A paramedic rushed past Doc. "Let me examine her. Put her down." Over his shoulder he spoke to Doc. "I need light."

Alex held on to Jade, gripped by dread that if he ever let go, she'd slip away for good.

"Agent." The paramedic put a hand on his arm. "You have to let me help her. Please—set her down."

"Alex." Doc's voice was gentle but firm.

Alex lifted his gaze to Doc's.

"You've got to release her to them. She's going to be fine."

"Promise me." Alex wasn't sure who he meant—Doc, medical personnel…God?

Finally, with a shudder, Alex relinquished her into the care of the medical team who'd arrived.

But not before he saw the somber expression that passed between them.

Doc placed one hand on his shoulder and squeezed.

The sympathy weakened him. He had to be strong for Jade. Had to believe.

Alex backed away and sank to his heels, gripping his hands.

And prayed.

Please. I'll do anything.

Even give her up.

Chapter Seventeen

Alex crouched against the hospital wall, as close to the surgical suite as he could get, and stared at the automatic doors that couldn't be opened from this side. His fingers flexed under the urge to tear them open with his bare hands.

"Here," Doc said from above him, proffering yet another cup of coffee.

His stomach lining was shot, but Alex accepted it, simply for something to do. Slowly, he rose to his feet.

His gaze remained on the doors.

"The Woods girl's family arrived to take her home. She'll be fine, the doctor said. Dehydrated and dirty, but otherwise okay."

"She should have counseling," Alex observed without looking at Doc.

"Yeah. She'll get it. Victims Services has already been in touch. She didn't want to leave until she was certain Jade was going to make it, but her parents insisted. I promised we'd call her when we knew more."

Jade, be strong. You have to pull through. No other option was bearable.

"Don't suppose it would do any good to tell you to go home and sleep."

Alex snorted. "Don't suppose."

"It wasn't your fault," Doc said. "Either time."

Alex's fingers crushed the Styrofoam cup. Hot coffee splashed his skin.

He barely felt it.

"Goddamn, Alex." Doc snatched the cup. "Go run some cold water over that."

Alex glanced at the hand as if it didn't belong to him. "It doesn't hurt." He wiped it on his jeans and returned to staring at the doors ahead.

Doc's mouth opened as if to reason with him. With a shake of his head, he halted. Clapped a hand against Alex's shoulder and squeezed. "When she comes out of there, forget about writing a report. You can do it when you return from vacation."

Alex tore his gaze away and blinked. "Vacation?" He gestured toward the surgical suite. "You've got to be kidding."

"You're treading the thin edge of exhaustion, friend, and it goes deeper than this case. You either take time off voluntarily or I have you suspended from duty. Your choice." He softened the demand. "Jade will need company, anyway."

"Jade will choose better company than me." Over and over, he watched the knife sweep downward, tearing precious white flesh—

While he, too late, fired his weapon.

Blood. So much blood on his hands. Why should she forgive him? He'd never forgive himself.

"We'll see," Doc remarked. "I think you're wrong."

When Alex didn't answer, Doc leaned against the wall beside him and settled in to wait.

Up…there. High. So…far.

Like a fish in a deep pool, she idly noted the light near the surface.

Can't. Tired.

A thought flitted past, gossamer…gone. An image. Something she…

Someone. She wanted…wanted…

Please. Stay. Where is…?

Warm golden…

She gathered herself to reach for—

Pushing, pushing, stretching—

Alex. Nowhere, nowhere, no…

Noise broke over her. She tensed. Stirred.

Frowned. *Hurts.*

And slipped back into the cool, welcoming darkness.

"You can see her." Doc's voice came to Alex as he stared out across the city, wondering how the sun could shine and people could drive and work and live when Jade was—

He whirled. "What?"

"They'll let you in, but only for a minute."

"She's—" The tight, cold fist around his heart eased its grip.

The nurse behind Doc spoke up. "Ms. Butler is in Recovery but will be in her ICU room in a few minutes. Doc says you're her fiancé, that she has no relatives."

Alex cast a startled glance at Doc, who winked. "Uh, yeah. Her parents are dead, and she has no siblings." He took a step toward the nurse. "How is she?"

The nurse nodded. "Follow me." They left Doc behind.

"The trauma surgeon had to remove her spleen and part of her liver. She's lost a lot of blood."

He halted. Clasped her arm. "She's going to be all right?"

"She survived the surgery. That means a lot. Ms. Butler has a long recuperation ahead of her, but it's in her favor that she's young and physically fit." The woman led him past several cubicles with glass walls. Outside each one was a nurse. Inside was a welter of equipment.

She paused in front of a doorway and indicated the woman working inside. "Each patient has her own nurse. Cindy is as good as they come." She patted his arm. "Wait until she finishes, and she'll give you an update."

Alex barely heard her or marked her departure. He only had eyes for Jade's red hair, spilled like blood over the white pillowcase.

Blood. Her blood on his fingers. Her face, parchment white—

He strode to the window and waited for the nurse to move, so he could catch a glimpse of Jade's face.

When he did, it was like a punch to the stomach. He pressed one palm against the glass.

Fragile again, like the young girl. Pale and bruised, a tube in her mouth, more in her arms.

Machines everywhere, a forest of them. *Jade, where are you?*

"You're Alex, right? I'm Cindy, Ms. Butler's nurse."

Alex jolted and turned to face her.

"It's hard," she said, "seeing them this way. She probably won't wake fully for several hours, but the ER nurse said she kept asking for you before they put her under. Make her aware that you're here, and it's likely to help. She can't talk because of the tube, but often patients can hear well before we can tell that they're waking."

He followed her to the bed, at a loss to know what to do.

He wanted to touch her, but—

"Contact helps, too. Just watch out for the paraphernalia." Then she stepped away. "I can only let you stay five minutes. I'm sorry. I'll be right outside."

So still. So…small. Unlike the Jade he knew, vibrant, always in motion, temperamental and rebellious—

"Come back," he whispered, and the sound of his voice somehow brought him back to reality. Five minutes wasn't enough. He slipped his hand over her fingers, careful to avoid the IV taped to the skin. With the other, he stroked her hair, and the thick silk of it somehow settled him because, at last, something felt like Jade.

He leaned down to her ear. "You can yell at me all you want, Jade. Kick my ass from here to Georgia. Tell me to go to hell, just—" His throat tightened. "Come back."

He inhaled, searching for the cinnamon-and-peaches scent of her, but it was buried beneath the sting of antiseptics. "Jade—" His voice caught, and he had to blink fast to clear his vision. "Please…I need to tell you—"

"Sir," the nurse interrupted gently. "I'm sorry. It's time. You can return in an hour."

He closed his eyes and squeezed Jade's fingers, then stepped away.

Just as well. He had no right to tell her that she was what he wanted most in the world, whether or not he deserved her.

He wouldn't force his love on her. She'd faced death twice and survived in spite of him.

The future must be her choice. He'd been part of the worst moments of her life; she might want nothing to do with a man so inextricably entwined with nightmares she could never fully erase.

He leaned down and pressed a kiss to her brow.

"Your call, sweetheart. Just…please…come back to me."

Thick…smothering. Need…air. Can't…breathe, can't—

"Sh-h. You're safe," said that voice from her dreams. "You're okay."

She relaxed at the sound of him.

Warm. Strong. Safe.

Alex. Something—have to—She tensed, trying to rise, to tell—

"Take it easy, sweetheart. You're safe. Just rest."

Eyes…heavy. Need to—

She gathered herself for one more push.

Open…please.

A hand squeezed hers. "That's right. Open your eyes, Jade. Talk to us."

Barely, she managed a glimpse. Golden. Tired.

Haunted. "Alex…"

"I'm here." The Voice meant safety. Hope.

"Hurts."

"I know. I'll get the nurse. Sleep now. Next time will be better."

"Want…" But before she could capture the words dancing away, her lids drifted shut again.

She thought she felt something warm brush her lips just before the darkness embraced her.

Alex spoke to the nurse, then left Jade's room and carefully made his way down a long, bright corridor toward the nurses' station.

"She's awake, huh? That's good news," called one of the several nurses with whom he'd become well-acquainted over the past three days. "Maybe now you can get some sleep."

Alex managed a nod but kept going, blindly rushing past other greetings, his pace increasing as he sought out the stairwell.

He hit the door and raced down to the next half level and under the railing.

There, in the shadows, he sank to his heels.

With a wordless shudder, the man known as The Sphinx dropped his head into his hands.

And wept.

Chapter Eighteen

"**R**eady?" Doc asked.

"Oh, yeah." Jade glanced around the room she couldn't wait to leave. Three days in ICU, then six here…she was more than ready to get home.

"Your chariot's on its way," Sean offered.

"I think I could walk on my own."

"Forget it. Even if they'd let you," Sean said "we won't. You're part of a team now, and we take care of our own."

Our own. Jade still couldn't believe that she'd earned a permanent spot on VICTAF once she was cleared for duty.

It hadn't been so hard to obtain, in the end—all she'd had to do was nearly die. Regardless, she was in and there was nothing anyone could do.

Not even Alex.

"Everyone's downstairs waiting," Doc said.

Her head rose swiftly. *Everyone?* She wanted to ask, but she wouldn't. He hadn't come to the hospital all those years before. She was surprised at the bitter sting of his absence.

Doc's eyes softened in understanding. "Almost everyone," he corrected. "I told you Alex took some time off."

"Doesn't matter." She averted her face and pretended to check once again for her belongings.

Meanwhile, the atmosphere in the room turned stiff and

uncomfortable.

"I don't care what he said," Sean blurted. "She should know, Doc."

She glanced up and saw the unspoken message wing between them. "Know what?"

Doc frowned. Sean looked mutinous. Finally, Doc sighed. "He was here, Jade. He didn't leave the hospital from the moment they brought you in until you woke up. For three days, he barely slept or ate. He didn't want anyone to tell you."

He'd come. "I heard his voice. I thought I imagined it." *You're safe.* "Why hide it?"

"Because he's The Sphinx," Sean said with disgust.

"No." Doc spoke softly. "He can't get past his sense of responsibility for putting you in that position."

"But he didn't—"

"I understand. I'm the one who chose you, and you were eager to volunteer, but none of that makes a difference to him. Alex's been in a lot of tight spots, and he's always been cool and unflappable. Nothing rattles him, but you have, Jade. Something in him died when you got hurt. After you disappeared, he would have dug out a mountain with his bare hands to find you. That night all those years ago—it haunts him, and then when you got hurt on his watch, well… It's just who he is. A protector to the bone, a lone wolf with a rigid sense of honor. He walked away precisely because he wants you so badly. He's not going to ask. Instead, he's giving you room to make your own choice."

She heard the nurse coming with the wheelchair. She grasped Doc's arm. "When will he be back?"

Doc and Sean traded glances again.

"What? Tell me."

Doc's shoulders sank. "He resigned."

"From VICTAF?"

He shook his head. "From the Bureau."

"What?" She blinked. "But he—"

"He's leaving town," Sean said.

Before she could learn more, the nurse arrived, and Jade was swept up in a small tornado of well-wishers. Nearly thirty minutes went by before she was safely ensconced in Doc's SUV.

"Put the seat back and nap while I'm driving you home," he said gently. "Everyone meant well, but you're worn out."

"No." She gripped the door handle. "I mean, I am, but—" She swallowed hard. "Take me to him, Doc. Please."

"Jade—"

"Please."

"You're in no shape—"

"I have to talk to him, and I'm afraid he won't—" *Wait for me. Come to me.* "Please, Doc."

"The home health people will be at your place soon."

"They'll keep. This won't."

Doc stared at her. Finally, he shook his head. "On one condition."

"What?"

"You don't set foot from this car." When she started to protest, he held up a hand. "My way or the highway, Detective. I can carry you to him or he can walk out to you, but you're not moving one more step until you get home. Take it or leave it."

Neither was ideal for the conversation she wanted to have with Alex, but she wasn't exactly in a position to insist. "You just like pulling rank," she muttered.

He grinned. "Power has its privileges, though damn few of them. Now, lie back and rest until we get there."

"You're the boss," she grumbled.

"Yep." He smiled. "I surely am." And with that, he pulled away from the curb.

Alex slid another painting into its crate and glanced around, tallying how many more he would need.

Something warm rubbed against his leg, and he peered down.

And smiled. "Hey, buddy."

Major's expressive eyes read worry.

"She'll be okay. I promise." Alex leaned over and bestowed a healthy scratching under the dog's chin.

Major sighed and leaned into him. Alex noted at all the packing left to do, then shrugged. It wasn't like he had an appointment to be anywhere.

He settled on the floor cross-legged and gave the animal a thorough rubbing. Then he heard footsteps.

Their parents were due in two days, but Rafe had driven down to Austin as soon as they'd heard. Long legs crossed the floor unsteadily as a result of near-fatal injuries sustained on Rafe's last mission. For a man no one thought would ever walk again, however, a limp was nothing.

He looked around. "Sure you don't want me to help pack?"

"I've hired movers. I just don't like anyone else crating the paintings."

"Alex, you're positive you're not going to regret this?" Rafe asked. "I mean, we're all tickled as hell to think of having you back home, but—" His eyes, a unique blend of blue and gray inherited from their Anglo mother, had always seen too much. It was part of what made Rafe such a powerful healer.

He seemed to perceive as much of the heart as the body and sense what to do with both. "You've been a cop for nearly twenty years. You know you're a good one. It's hard to walk away from who you are."

His brother understood that better than most. He'd been a rising star in the army when his career was abruptly cut short, and finding his new path hadn't come easily.

"I'm..." Alex searched for the description. "Weary, I guess." He gestured toward the paintings. "Someone told me recently that it was a crime that I wasn't doing this full-time, that these should be in a gallery."

"She's right."

Alex's head whipped around. "What makes you think it was a she?"

"Your voice." Rafe smiled sadly. "I can't argue with her—your talent has always amazed me." Which was saying something, coming from a man whose pottery could steal the breath. "But what about leaving her? She's the one, isn't she?"

"Don't—" Alex's tone hardened. "It's complicated and—" He shook his head. "I'm not ready to talk about it yet."

A knock sounded at the front door. Major's ears perked up, and he trotted out of the room.

"Must be our pizza. I'll get it," Rafe said. But before he left, he squeezed his brother's shoulder. "Whenever you want to talk, I'm happy to listen."

"Thanks." Alex watched them go, then returned to his packing.

Jade watched from the car as Doc knocked and the door opened.

But it wasn't Alex inside. A tall, handsome dark-haired man opened the door and—

A black streak shot across the lawn.

"Major!" Jade opened her door, and he scrambled inside, whimpering and licking as she clutched him and cried. "Oh, sweetie, I missed you so much." She buried her face in his fur and held on tight.

"He's a great dog," said a deep, amused voice.

She glanced over to see strong features that reminded her of—

"You're Rafe."

Doc spoke up then. "He is. Rafe, this is Jade Butler. She's—"

"Alex's woman trouble," Rafe interrupted, his silvery eyes solemn now. "You mean to turn my brother's life upside down?"

"Me? I'm not—" She snapped her gaping mouth shut. "No. Not that it's any of your business. Your brother's no angel, you know. He's got a lot to answer for. He—"

To her surprise, Rafe burst out laughing and held up a hand. "Whoa." His eyes were bright with humor. "I think my little brother just met his match." He traded smiles with Doc. "About time."

"Where is he?"

The cheer faded. "In the house. He'd say he doesn't want to see you."

She wouldn't let that hurt. Her chin tilted up. "Then he shouldn't have kidnapped my dog."

The corners of Rafe's mouth curved. "My mother's going to love you."

His words reminded Jade of what was at stake. Fear tightened her fingers on Major's coat, and the dog whined. "She might not ever meet me if I don't do this right."

"I've never witnessed my brother scared before, but you've got him spooked. He's always loaded too much on his shoulders. Sounds like this time, the weight's about to buckle his knees." Rafe's eyes warmed. "Maybe you can remove some of it."

"I told him I didn't need him to take care of me."

"Join the club. He listen?"

She shook her head. "I nearly got both of us killed." She frowned. "It wasn't his fault. It was mine."

He peered at Jade. "I'm thinking Doc and Major can hang out here and shoot the breeze with me if you want to go inside."

"She was just discharged from the hospital," Doc said. "She needs to go home to bed."

"If I don't walk in there on my own two feet, he'll just keep beating himself up, Doc. I've gone a longer distance than this in the hallways."

The expert eyes of a healer scanned her. Jade held her breath.

"No dizziness? Shortness of breath?" Rafe asked.

"No."

"How's your pain level?"

"Two," she answered in the hospital scale of one to ten.

Rafe frowned slightly, then looked at Doc. "I'd carry her if my leg would handle it." He considered her. "Let Doc cart you to the door, then you can walk the rest of the way yourself." He paused. "But sit down as soon as you find him. He's in his studio."

"Thank you." She hugged Major. "I'll be back, okay?"

Major woofed.

When Doc picked her up, she caught Rafe's gaze. "Wish me luck."

He nodded. "For both of you."

Once in the house, she moved slowly through the living room and down the hallway. Just outside the door to his studio, she drew a deep breath to settle her nerves and peered inside.

Alex stood in front of the easel, staring at a canvas in his hands. His entire frame spoke of exhaustion.

Then he set the painting back. "You and the pizza guy have a—"

At the sight of her, he went stock-still, his gaze riveted on her.

She drank in every detail. "You're tired."

He blinked and stirred. Took a step forward. "What are you doing here?"

She didn't answer, caught by the image behind him. She opened her mouth to speak, but couldn't find the words, so she merely pointed.

She recognized the top corner, which was all she'd glimpsed of the painting he'd hastily stashed on that unforgettable night they'd shared.

It was a painting of her as she'd never imagined herself.

"Beautiful," she whispered. She looked... "Strong. Powerful." One step, then another until she stood right in front of an enchantress with long auburn waves cascading over the bodice of a filmy pale green gown. Slender ribbons of gold crossed her shoulders and wrapped beneath her breasts, then looped once more to form a girdle at her hips from which hung a jeweled scabbard bearing the carved handle of a knife.

The gown revealed nearly as much as it concealed, and the siren had both abundant curves and well-toned muscle. She was regal. Potent. Dramatic.

And sexy. A charged eroticism permeated every brush

stroke. This was a woman who would yield only when she wished, a demanding lover, a woman at the height of her powers. Part sorceress, part queen.

Never victim.

He'd understood, better than she, the woman she'd tried so hard to become.

"You should sit down," he said finally.

Jade shook her head. "No."

"Jade, don't be foolish. You're recovering from serious injuries."

"The worst of which you inflicted on me."

He recoiled from the blow. "I know that. Sit down." He moved to an old ratty sofa in the corner and cleared it.

"No. You don't understand, Alex. I'm not talking about Dan or Kirk or anything physical." She dodged his grasp. "And I'm not sitting down. Not yet."

She pointed to the painting. "If I let you coddle me, you'll never see me that way, and you'll keep trying to protect me from the world."

"No. I won't. I'm through with that." He clenched his jaw. "I've failed twice in a pretty spectacular way and nearly gotten you killed both times."

"Oh, bugger that," she snapped.

His head jerked up. "What?"

"You heard me." She closed the gap between them and jabbed a finger into his chest. "We're not doing that anymore, Alex—at least, I'm not. You take things too seriously."

He glared, but she pressed on. "You can live in the past if that's your cup of tea, but you won't make me do it. Twice now I've thought my future was over. I'm going to live to the fullest and grab everything I want most and hang on." She paused for a second to wrestle her temper under control.

"It's just my stupid bad luck that what I most want in the

world—" she glared right back "—is you."

The fury in his eyes blinked out in a dumbfounded instant. "What did you say?"

"Are you going deaf, or are you just not listening to me?" Her throat crowded with frustration and longing and an urge to scream.

Instead, to her utter mortification, she burst into tears. "Damn you, Alex Sandoval. You're not easy to love, you know that? I can't imagine how your family puts up with you."

He gaped at her, speechless for once.

"Oh, great—now you have nothing to say. I've just spilled my guts and you—" She stabbed again. "You—"

All of a sudden, the bottom dropped out of her. "I think I should sit—" Her head spun—

He caught her as she crumpled and swung her into his arms. Raced into the living room, shouting for his brother. "Rafe—quick—"

"I'm here." Rafe stepped in the front door. "Set her down."

"She—oh, God—"

"Lay her on the couch, Alex." He spoke gently. "Let me look at her."

"Doc, call 911." Alex gripped her hand but leaped to his feet, adrenaline surging.

"No need," Rafe said while examining her. "She just fainted. See? She's coming around."

Alex dropped back to his knees and leaned over her.

Mossy green eyes fluttered open. Jade lifted her hand to his face and smiled. "Alex. You're here." She glanced around at the faces above her. "What—?"

He saw memory return. Her gaze narrowed and clicked to him. "Where was I? Oh, yeah—I'm mad at you."

His heart finally resumed its rhythm. "No, you're not. You said you love me."

Rafe chuckled. "Diana's never had trouble doing both."

"Butt out, bro." Alex's gaze flicked up to Doc. "Same to you." He glanced over at the dog. "Major can stay."

"I'm not going anywhere," Rafe said. "I have to record this for posterity as the family representative. If I could paint it, I'd title this picture *Alex Meets His Match*."

Alex fought a grin as he returned his gaze to Jade. "Ignore them."

She fluttered her lashes. "Maybe if I had a distraction."

He laughed then as relief soared. He bent to place a soft kiss on her lips, his heart lighter than it had been in years. Twelve, to be exact.

"That'll work." She slid her fingers into his hair and deepened the kiss.

Rafe rose slowly and nodded to Doc. "We'll just be outside, won't we, Doc? Come on, Major."

After they left, Alex drew back and clasped her fingers in his. "If I reminded you that I'm too old for you—"

"I'd whip my knife from my scabbard—" She broke off, appalled, as she saw the memory of Dan Fleming intervene. "Don't," she pleaded. "I didn't mean—"

Alex touched her throat where one still-healing scar lined her precious flesh. "I know." He swallowed. "But it's hard to forget seeing you...your blood..." He bowed his head and gripped her hand.

Jade smoothed her fingers over his hair. "Alex, I'll turn down the VICTAF slot if you'll come back. You're more important to them than I am."

His head rose swiftly. "No. You're wrong. I'm—" He glanced away, then back. "I'm through, Jade. Maybe I'll want to return to law enforcement later, but right now I only want…"

"What? Tell me." She laid her hand on his jaw.

His golden eyes caressed her. "Two things. You—that's not negotiable. The second is."

Jade smiled and squeezed his fingers. "I like the first one. What else?"

"Okay, three, really. You and…kids—you want kids, Jade?"

"Oh, yeah. You bet I do."

"Major thinks this yard is great. The house has enough room for the first baby, maybe more. You like this place, Jade?"

Her eyes glowed. "Oh, yes." She sobered. "But what's number three?"

He thought she probably already knew. "I might not be good enough, but—" He drew a deep breath. "I want to see if I can make a living painting instead of squeezing in an hour or two here and there."

"You can." Her smile was smug.

"Pretty cocky when it's not your heart on display, aren't you?"

"You think my heart wasn't hanging way over the cliff when I walked into your studio a little while ago? You believe I wasn't terrified?"

Alex shook his head. "You had more courage at fifteen than most grown men." With a deep sigh, he drew her into his arms. "Will you be my woman, Jade Butler?" he said into her ear. "The queen of my heart?"

"Will you stop telling me you're not my hero, Alex Sandoval?" She leaned back and stared solemnly into his eyes. "You were and are, and nothing you say will change my mind."

Then she laughed, free and delighted.

"What is it?"

"I told you once that in my secret thoughts, I always thought of you as The Voice back then." Her cheeks bloomed with color. "I was just thinking about having The Voice whispering in my ear every night of my life." Mischief chased over her features. "And then I learned that they called you The Sphinx at VICTAF." Her lips curved in a flirtatious smile. "Think The Sphinx might want to talk dirty to me in bed?"

He swept her up in his arms and strode toward his bedroom. "You're not ready for anything but sleep right now, Detective." He cast her a devil's grin. "But once you're back in fighting trim, well..." He lifted one dark eyebrow. "It's for me to know and you to find out."

He pressed his mouth to hers. "But here's a clue."

He whispered in her ear as he kicked the door shut behind them.

And Jade laughed.

Epilogue

T he next day, the house overflowed with family.

Jade, imprisoned on the sofa, much to her disgruntlement, lay back against Alex's chest and marveled. "I always wanted this," she said softly.

"Hmm?" Alex roused himself from playing with her hair. "Wanted what?"

"This," she gestured. "A great big, messy family."

"Mom—" Carrying his bright-eyed daughter, Liam Sullivan called out behind himself. "Jade just insulted your kids." His eyes sparkled, and he was so gorgeous she had to remind herself to breathe.

Even if he did look exhausted.

"I did not—" She tried to sit up straight, but Alex locked a strong arm around her.

"Whoa, tiger. I'm telling you, hotshot, she'll whip your ass when she's back on her feet. Don't mess with my detective."

"Little pitchers," Liam reminded him, clapping his hands over his daughter's ears.

Gracie spotted Major and dove. "Ga!"

Liam barely caught her. She squirmed on his lap, reaching out for the patient animal. "Sorry, dude," he said to Major. "You're her fatal attraction, but I'll protect you." He settled on the floor with Gracie, who squealed and aimed her little

226

body like an arrow.

Raina approached and sat cross-legged on the other side of the dog. "Softly, sweetie. See, like this?" She stroked Major's fur, and the dog's expressive eyes turned up to her as if pleading.

Gracie tried to push to standing and grunted, her intent clear as she held out her arms.

Alex had to laugh. "She's as bull-headed as her father. He would never take no for an answer."

"Hey!" Liam protested, juggling her and keeping her from her goal.

Gracie protested, then turned her face up to her father, bottom lip stuck out and a tear wobbling on her lashes.

"Oh, God, don't do that," Liam pleaded. He closed his eyes. "Tears. I can't take it."

"Sap," said Jilly from behind him. She bent over his shoulder. "Way to go, honey. Tears get them every time."

Raina laughed then, and Jade saw Liam's attention turn to her as though it was a sound he couldn't hear enough. Alex had told her a little about the woman who had suffered such tragedy.

Then Liam glared at his sister. "You're not turning her into a spoiled brat like yourself." But his eyes were twinkling as he complained.

Raina took her daughter and settled her between her legs, patiently teaching her to pet Major gently.

Mostly Grace patted with perhaps a little too much enthusiasm, but Major bore it stoically.

"Is my scapegrace son bothering your poor dog, Jade?" Celeste approached.

"Hey—" Liam protested. "I'm a respectable husband and father now."

"Reconsider, Raina," said the sister Alex had made safe.

Jilly bumped against her brother's shoulder. "I'm telling you, he's like milk. After a while he turns rotten."

"Zip your lip, kid, or I'll start telling little Jilly stories," Liam warned.

And then they were off, competing with affectionate, teasing anecdotes about each other. Jade leaned back against Alex's chest and whispered in his ear. "At least three."

"What?" He glanced down. "Oh. Well…" He waggled his eyebrows. "We'd better get started." And sealed his mouth to hers.

"Careful," Diana said, settling at the other end of the sofa, patting her still-flat belly. "That's how this began."

Rafe sat on the arm. "Yeah, but the practicing was a lot of fun."

"Wait, what?" Alex sat up. "Are you saying you two are going to have a baby?"

His very serious brother nodded, his face alight as he wrapped his wife's shoulders.

Jade turned and saw Alex's features soften. "That's awesome, bro. No one deserves the happiness more."

Through the excited chatter rising, Hal spoke up. "Did you say I'm going to be a grandfather again?" Hal turned to his wife. "You hear that, sweetheart?"

Celeste's eyes misted, and she approached her oldest son. "I did. Oh, Rafe, I'm so happy for you." She took Diana's hands. "What a blessing. When are you due?"

"Six months from now," Diana answered. "We didn't want to say anything until we'd passed that first trimester."

"You hear that, pumpkin?" Liam leaned toward his little girl. "You're gonna have a cousin." He rose and went to Rafe. "Welcome to the land of the sleep-deprived." He slapped his brother's back, then bent to kiss Diana's cheek. "You're gonna be a great mom, Doc."

Diana bit her lip. "I want to be."

Rafe kissed her hair. "You will. I have no doubts."

"Does Abuelita know?" Alex asked.

Diana's cheeks colored. "She figured it out before I did. Some doctor, huh?"

Alex grinned. "She's always a step ahead of all of us."

"So…you two. You're getting married?" Diana smiled at them.

They traded looks. "I just now got him to admit he's not robbing the cradle," Jade responded, "so it might take a bit to—"

"Yeah," Alex interrupted. "We are." He glanced at her. "At least, that's what I want." There was so much love in his gaze that Jade felt herself blushing.

"Me, too," she replied softly. "Wow."

Their gazes locked, both of them with growing smiles.

"This house would make a good home," Diana said.

Jade closed her eyes against the strength of her longing. "I love it."

"What about you, big brother?" Liam asked. "You already packed."

Alex was still embracing her with his eyes. "I can unpack."

"It holds a lot of wonderful memories," Diana said. "They were happy here. I know it would make them feel great to have a new family being sheltered under this roof."

Shelter, Jade thought. A home of her own, the one she'd wished for, with that white picket fence. The man of her dreams making the life she'd longed for but never really thought she'd have.

"You were going home to La Paloma," she said to Alex.

"Where you are will be my home from now."

"You'll still be family," Celeste said. "And you'll come

visit."

"Family," she breathed.

Raina nodded, as if she understood the yearning. "It's the best family you could ever imagine being part of."

Jade glanced around at all of them, then over at Alex.

He was smiling, but his eyes were serious, as if making a vow. "Let me share my family. There's always room for one more, right?" He glanced up at the many loving faces watching them.

"Absolutely, son," Hal boomed.

"After years of torture by these brothers, I need all the sisters I can get," Jilly teased.

Diana smiled at her. "Raina is right. I understand being alone in the world, too. You'll never be alone again, and you'll never find better."

Jade could barely see through the tears that suddenly swamped her as she turned back to Alex. "I'd love that, more than you can imagine."

Relief rose in his features. "I can imagine a lot. And I love you." He pulled her close and kissed her.

"Ga!" Gracie squealed and clapped.

The rest of the family laughed and joined her.

~THE END~

Thank you for letting me share my stories with you!

Next up in Sweetgrass Springs is BE MINE THIS CHRISTMAS, a Christmas novella.

Gib Douglas has been on the road a long time, with no place to really call home. When he pays a holiday visit to relatives in Sweetgrass Springs, the last person he expects to encounter is the girl he loved, the girl who'd promised to marry him and love him forever...until she betrayed him and married someone else.

Dulcie Maguire gave up her dreams so that Gib could follow his all those years ago. She made a decent life for herself while watching him soar to success with great pride, never expecting to see him again. Now widowed, she's in dire straits with four children depending on her, when into her life walks Gib again—and she realizes that she's never gotten over him.

But the man he's become is not the boy she once knew—and he may never forgive her, once he knows the secret she's been concealing.

If you liked TEXAS PROTECTOR, there are two earlier stories in the Lone Star Lovers trilogy, Alex's brother Liam Sullivan's story, TEXAS HEARTTHROB and their brother Rafe's story, TEXAS HEALER. The other books in the TEXAS HEROES series are listed further below.

Hollywood's hottest heartthrob Liam Sullivan has escaped the paparazzi and celebrity gossips after a sensational tragedy, reexamining his high-flying lifestyle and his priorities. In disguise, traveling through the Smoky Mountains of North Carolina, he encounters a rail-thin, starving woman who has lost everything but the dilapidated cabin where she once lived with her grandmother in happier days. Raina Donovan is determined to make her stand there, but winter is coming, and Liam cannot desert her until he can make her safe, however much she tries to make him leave.

Day by day, they draw closer, but Raina has secrets and so does Liam. Before they can trust enough to confide in each other, the world catches up with them. Can they overcome the stunning shock of their deceptions to find a way to be together, or will the price of their lies ruin any chance they might have for a future?

"Jean Brashear's portrait of two wounded souls who find each other just when they most need someone is beautifully, gently drawn. Brashear's smooth style and attention to detail make [this] quietly captivating."

~RTBookclub (4½ of 5 stars)

Start reading TEXAS HEARTTHROB today!

Brilliant and driven cardiac surgeon Diana Morgan's whole life centers around her career, now threatened by an injury that may prove insurmountable. She is desperate enough to accept a forced sabbatical to the Davis Mountains of West Texas, where she meets Rafael Sandoval, a former Special Forces medic who understands exactly how it feels to have the life you planned taken from you. After losing his men and nearly losing his life, Rafe has returned home and found a measure of peace combining his Western medical training with the curanderismo or folk healing traditions of his Latino heritage.

Diana desperately needs the healing Rafe is dedicated to providing, but his hard-won peace is threatened by the growing attachment neither welcomes. Too many people in his valley count on him for the only medical help available for many miles, and too many lives back in her world— one he once wanted with everything in him—will be lost if she cannot regain her skills. But healing her means losing her, for she can't stay in his world…and he can't leave.

"Jean Brashear's knack for storytelling shines in a poignant romance about two people traveling different

paths to the same destination, to heal, to comfort and to love."

Start reading TEXAS HEALER today!

If you enjoyed TEXAS PROTECTOR, I would be very grateful if you would help others find this book by recommending it to your friends on Goodreads or by writing a review. If you would like to be informed when my next release is available, please sign up for my newsletter by visiting my website at www.jeanbrashear.com.

I love hearing from you, so please contact me through any of the options at the end of this book.

Thanks!

Jean

Please enjoy this excerpt from TEXAS HEARTTHROB:

Prologue

Manhattan

"Liam, is it true that you and Gisella had a secret wedding last weekend in Cancún?" the blond reporter from the *Star* shouted. The noise level rocketed as camera crews and microphones crowded the hotel ballroom at the press conference for Liam Sullivan's latest film.

Liam resisted a groan. He'd known that the snapshot of him with the supermodel would be fresh meat for the tabloids. "Thanks for the vote of confidence, Heather, but I just met the woman a week ago when we attended the same preview party." He winked. "I'm sure a famous beauty like her can do better than some ole small-town Texas boy."

The assembled reporters hooted. The blonde named

Heather batted her eyelashes at him. Fresh off an Oscar nomination and just named "Sexiest Man Alive" by *People* magazine, Liam Sullivan was the hottest star in Hollywood at the moment. Life was sweet. He was enjoying the heck out of it, but the man who'd been a skinny, brainy runt of the litter was only too aware of what life could be like on the flip side of good looks and fame. And if he forgot, his older brothers Rafael, Alejandro and Dane would gladly bring him back to earth.

He missed them, missed his mother and father, his pesky younger sister, Jilly. Two more stops on this publicity tour for his new release, then he had six weeks off before his next film. He couldn't wait to head home to Texas and hibernate for a while.

As the director fielded questions, Liam listened with half an ear, scanning the crowd without really seeing. He was so tired. His ex-girlfriend Kelly's middle-of-the-night call had kept him tossing in his bed. They hadn't been an item in months, not since he'd finally realized that she didn't want to kick her cocaine habit, that no matter what help he offered, she wasn't ready to accept. It frustrated the hell out of him. The waste of it sickened him. He'd seen too many people in his business dragged down by the fast life. Kelly was well on her way to being another casualty, no matter how hard Liam had fought to save her.

"Liam has no comment on that."

The tension in his publicist Annie Schaefer's voice alerted Liam that he'd missed a question.

That the room had fallen unnaturally silent.

"So she's just another disposable girlfriend?" jeered a voice from the back.

"What?" Liam turned to Annie. "What's he talking about?"

"Get up and leave—now," she whispered, hand over

Liam's microphone. "I'll handle this."

Liam almost obeyed—he'd had plenty of experience with the landmines the press could plant—but something in the gathering buzz of the audience, something about the shock in Annie's eyes, kept him in place. "Tell me what's going on," he demanded.

A reporter spoke up first. "Her brother says it's your fault, Liam. That Kelly Mason killed herself because you abandoned her when she told you she was pregnant. Not exactly what we've come to expect from All-American Liam Sullivan, is it?"

Dead? Liam couldn't speak. Kelly...*pregnant?* His mind went white. How could—Last night she'd cried on the phone but refused to tell him why. She'd begged him to come back, but she'd been high and hysterical and—

He jerked the mike toward him. "When she called, she never mentioned—"

The buzz leaped to a roar.

"You mean she called you before she did it?"

"What did you say to make her kill herself?"

"You didn't want the baby?"

How could it be his? They hadn't made love in—

Annie grabbed the mike back. "This news comes as a terrible shock to all of us. Mr. Sullivan will have a statement later." She flipped off the microphone, nudging him none too gently to his feet. "You know better than to hand them something like that. Let's get out of here."

"But—" Liam looked out at the crowd as though somewhere in it lay the answers.

"Forget them—" she snapped. "They're piranhas, ready to feed." Her tone gentled. "You're rattled. I don't blame you. I'll phone some sources from the suite, see what I can find out."

He turned blind eyes to her. "She never said—" He glanced away. "I didn't let her finish. I thought it was just the same old—"

The crowd still clamored, shouting questions as he walked through the door in a daze.

He'd hung up on Kelly in disgust only hours ago. Given up on her, at last.

In so doing, had he driven her to give up on herself?

Chapter One

Two weeks later, a man who looked very little like Liam Sullivan drove down the deserted road he'd taken off the Blue Ridge Parkway on his way south to Asheville. Brushing an unfamiliar, newly-dark mustache with one finger, hair shaggy and no longer blond, he contemplated the dense thickets of rhododendron, the towering beeches and maples bearing hints of coming scarlet and gold. The Appalachians were ancient compared with the mountains he knew out West, and time had been a pumice stone, wearing steep peaks down to round, blue-shadowed waves extending as far as he could see. Near at hand, endless green slopes on either side of the road would break for a bald knob of charcoal rock.

Stunning, it was, but almost too rich for the eye. With a sudden ache, he longed for the starkness of the Davis Mountains of Texas, which were home.

His parents and siblings had called him every day since Kelly's death. Abuelita, the wise old healer who was as much his grandmother as if they shared genes, had even made one of her rare forays on the telephone, performing a long-distance diagnosis.

"*Cielito,*" she'd said. *Little sky*, the pet name she'd given him as a child. She'd always said his sunny nature made her think of a cloudless sky, *cielito sin nuves*. "Come home. You should be with those who love you." Ordering him, in no uncertain terms, to present himself with all haste for a *limpia*, or spiritual cleansing.

His sky was no longer cloudless; he had blood on his hands that would never wash out. Thank God Kelly's brother had been lying about her being pregnant, but that relief didn't lessen Liam's responsibility for her death. He carried the weight of it on his chest until he couldn't sleep at night for the smothering press of it.

He should have realized the last episode was different. He should have stopped her. Should have—

All the reassurances others offered dissolved to nothing in the face of knowing that he was the last person who had spoken to Kelly, the one to whom she'd reached out while her demons dug their claws into her throat and choked the life out of her. He could hardly remember the sunny, energetic starlet whose joy had attracted him so on the set of his first big hit.

Damn drugs. Try as he might, he could not understand how a person could know the damage they wreaked and still keep using them. He'd been there for Kelly, paid for rehab twice, would gladly have spent whatever necessary to fix her.

But he couldn't understand what it was that needed fixing, not really. Life threw things at you. You dealt with them. Sure, a beer now and then was nice, but—

Too damn wholesome, Liam, a friend had leveled the charge once. *You've never been tested in your entire charmed life.*

It was true. His half-brother Rafael had almost died in a Special Forces ambush and still bore scars and a limp. His other half-brother, Alejandro, was a hostage negotiator, had seen the darker side of life in his years in law enforcement. Even his photographer brother, Dane, had faced dangerous animals and treacherous mountain peaks.

And here Liam was, with more money and women than any man should have, simply because of his looks. Dodging only reporters, not bullets. Disguising himself with dark-brown dye on hair long past its usual razor cut, he was reduced to driving down back roads, seeking some time to think without the constant questions, the screaming headlines.

His brothers were the heroes. He just played them.

Ladyville, the sign up ahead said. Gratefully, Liam turned from pondering the demise of the All-American Boy to wondering if this burg would have a café where he could take a leak and grab a bite to eat. His jeans were loose on his waist, the casualty of too many sleepless nights and no appetite.

He hadn't even been able to attend the funeral to say goodbye to Kelly for fear of turning it into a circus. Her grieving family had deserved better.

Suddenly, Liam longed for his own family, wanted a taste of his mother's biscuits badly enough to whip the car around and catch the nearest plane to Texas. Wanted to forget the time alone he'd thought he needed and instead sit in her sunny kitchen and let her fuss over him, listen to his kid sister Jilly's early-morning grumbles. Walk out to the barn and hook a boot heel over a fence while comparing notes on the livestock with his dad.

But home was a good eighteen hundred miles away yet, and he had to buy gas and make a pit stop. This one-horse town was no bigger than tiny La Paloma, where Abuelita and Rafael lived, and there'd be nowhere to spend the night. Best to gas up and go, then get serious about heading straight to Texas in the morning.

That decided, he swerved into the parking lot of the only store in Ladyville and pulled up to the lone pump.

…Excerpt from TEXAS HEARTTHROB *by Jean Brashear* ©
2016

TEXAS HEARTTHROB
TEXAS HEALER
TEXAS PROTECTOR

Readers react to the
TEXAS HEROES series:

"In all of Jean's books so far I love the strong independent heroines and the men who know right away these women are special and fall in love in such a sweet way. Loving this series and can't wait to read more."

"Love the seamless flow from one book to another. Jean Brashear's Texas Heroes series is well worth a read. The characters are vivid and so real...the storylines are captivating. You won't go wrong purchasing this series."

"Jean Brashear, you are now one of my favorite authors. I loved them all and I can't wait to read some of your other books. You have the unique talent of making the reader feel like they have been transported to Texas and are part of the family. I found it very difficult to put down your books. Thank you for giving me hours of reading pleasure."

The Gallaghers of Morning Star

TEXAS SECRETS
TEXAS LONELY
TEXAS BAD BOY

"Jean Brashear's distinctive storytelling voice instantly draws in the reader. She writes with warmth and emotional truth."

~#1 NY Times bestselling author Debbie Macomber

"Jean is a fabulous writer that draws you in and has you laughing and crying and every emotion that there is. I love her and am going to buy the next set of books straight away."

"This is a must read trilogy if you love a love story with all the ingredients to make you laugh and cry and rejoice…loved it xxx"

The Marshalls

TEXAS REFUGE
TEXAS STAR
TEXAS DANGER

"Ms. Brashear has written a great story line with characters who are both 'larger than life' in some ways and yet very likeable, believable people. I'm looking forward to getting the next one about Quinn's brother, Josh, who is also in this book. Ms Brashear does indeed write very much like my most favorite author, Linda Howard."

"The Marshall men are quite spectacular and what they will do for the women they love wow! Not only are these men handsome, passionate, nurturing, but they will do anything to protect their families. Great books!"

"Jean Brashear will knock your socks off!"

The Gallaghers of Sweetgrass Springs

TEXAS ROOTS
TEXAS WILD
TEXAS DREAMS
TEXAS REBEL
TEXAS BLAZE
TEXAS CHRISTMAS BRIDE

"This was a fantastic series! The Gallaghers are a crazy bunch but have a heart of gold. The love each one has will be forever! I highly recommend this series!"

~Reader review

"Wow!! What a way to bring us back to the Texas Heroes series. Every time I read one of Jean's books about Sweetgrass Springs it makes me want to find this town and become a member. Catching up with the characters in the past books and seeing how new ones are written into the story lines is what keeps me coming back."

~Reader review

"I love taking trips to Sweetgrass Springs! The characters and the story draw you in and won't let you put the book down until you've read the happily ever after. The writing is excellent and I really love the small town setting!"

~Reader review

"Sweetgrass Springs, Texas embodies a special place for hearts that need healing. This warm and romantic series only gets better with each story, as all the characters we have come to love, from the beginning, move forward with their lives."

~Reader review

The Book Babes Trilogy

TEXAS TIES (Part One)
TEXAS TROUBLES (Part Two)
TEXAS TOGETHER (Part Three)

"I love the concept of this story, about a unique group of women whose friendship cements them, despite their differences. How they grow into their relationships, as the years pass, becoming stronger as they find new challenges, is compelling."

~Reader review

"Great start to what will be an awesome trilogy. I love the eclectic group of characters. All these strong women & some delicious men. I love the connection to Sweetgrass as well."

~Reader review

More Sweetgrass Springs Stories

TEXAS HOPE
TEXAS STRONG
TEXAS SWEET
BE MINE THIS CHRISTMAS

"You will laugh, cry but most of all enjoy the love this story is filled with. A truly heartwarming story that will leave an impression on you! A great series!"

~Reader review

"This latest story from the Sweetgrass Spring series is the most touching and heartwarming yet. Beautiful story of redemption."

~Reader review

"Oh boy, I just fell in love so hard. Tank is so damaged. I cried for the boy he was and the broken man he became. Chrissy is so feisty and has the heart of a lion. And she needs it, to help heal Tank. I think Jean Brashear's writing just keeps getting better & better. What a powerful story of love & healing. So beautiful."

~Reader review

"I must admit that I did tear up a bit with this one, but loved each of these people and their search for love and forgiveness. It's a MUST read."

~Reader review

"I can't say enough good things about Jean Brashear's books, I have read each and every one, and have loved them all. This one takes a hold of your heart and won't let go. It has the characters of her other books, but there is enough description in it that it can stand alone. The characters are so well developed that you feel like you know each one of them. I for one would love to find the town of Sweetgrass Springs and live there for the rest of my life. The mystery surrounding the family is so well developed, you feel like that you know them personally, and I can't wait for the next book."

~Reader review

* * *

About the Author

New York Times and *USAToday* bestselling Texas romance author of the popular TEXAS HEROES series and over 40 other novels in romance and women's fiction, a five-time RITA finalist and RT BOOKReviews Career Achievement Award winner, Jean Brashear knows a lot about taking crazy chances. A lifelong avid reader, at the age of forty-five with no experience and no training, she decided to see if she could write a book. It was a wild leap that turned her whole life upside down, but she would tell you that though she's never been more terrified, she's never felt more exhilarated or more alive. She's an ardent proponent of not putting off your dreams until that elusive 'someday'—take that leap now.

Connect With Jean

Visit Jean's website: www.jeanbrashear.com
Facebook: www.facebook.com/AuthorJeanBrashear
Twitter: www.twitter.com/@JeanBrashear
Pinterest: www.pinterest.com/bejeantx
Instagram: www.instagram.com/jeanbrashear

To be notified of new releases, sign up for Jean's newsletter on her website

Made in the USA
Middletown, DE
30 December 2016